SHERLOCK HOLMES AND THE KING'S GOVERNESS

Recent Titles by Barrie Roberts

SHERLOCK HOLMES and the RAILWAY MANIAC
SHERLOCK HOLMES and the DEVIL'S GRAIL
SHERLOCK HOLMES and the MAN FROM HELL
SHERLOCK HOLMES and the ROYAL FLUSH
SHERLOCK HOLMES and the HARVEST OF DEATH
SHERLOCK HOLMES and the CROSBY MURDERS
SHERLOCK HOLMES and the RULE OF NINE *
SHERLOCK HOLMES and the KING'S GOVERNESS *

* *available from Severn House*

SHERLOCK HOLMES AND THE KING'S GOVERNESS

Barrie Roberts

This first world edition published in Great Britain 2005 by
SEVERN HOUSE PUBLISHERS LTD of
9–15 High Street, Sutton, Surrey SM1 1DF.
This first world edition published in the USA 2005 by
SEVERN HOUSE PUBLISHERS INC of
595 Madison Avenue, New York, N.Y. 10022.

3 1558 00216 7823

British Library Cataloguing in Publication Data

Roberts, Barrie, 1939-
    Sherlock Holmes and the king's governess
    1.   Holmes, Sherlock (Fictitious character) - Fiction
    2.   Watson, John H. (Fictitious character) - Fiction
    3.   Detective and mystery stories
    I.   Title
    823.9'14 [F]

ISBN 0-7278-6223-5

Typeset by Palimpsest Book Production Ltd.,
Polmont, Stirlingshire, Scotland.
Printed and bound in Great Britain by
MPG Books Ltd., Bodmin, Cornwall.

Introduction

The text of this narrative is an edited version of a document which came into my possession some years ago. It appears to be one of the 'lost' or suppressed manuscripts of John H. Watson, the companion and chronicler of Sherlock Holmes. Watson was a contemporary of my maternal grandfather in the Medical Corps during the Great War and it may be through that connection that these papers came into the possession of my family.

I have already put several of these manuscripts before the public – *Sherlock Holmes and the Railway Maniac* (Constable, 1994), *Sherlock Holmes and the Devil's Grail* (Constable, 1996), *Sherlock Holmes and the Man From Hell* (Constable, 1997), *Sherlock Holmes and the Royal Flush* (Constable, 1999), *Sherlock Holmes and the Harvest of Death* (Constable, 2001), *Sherlock Holmes and the Crosby Murder* (Constable, 2002) and *Sherlock Holmes and the Rule of Nine* (Severn House, 2003), as well as a number of shorter ones which have mostly appeared in *The Strand Magazine* (USA).

Before seeking publication, I have made such checks as I have been able on the authenticity of the document. No unimpeachable example of Watson's handwriting exists, though those who claim expertise on the point have said that the writing is as likely to be his as not, and certainly the manuscript embodies the usual Watsonian mixture of real and invented personal and place names.

There are matters mentioned in the text which appear to confirm its authenticity, and some of these are discussed in my notes at the end of the book. It is entirely possible that some would bear deeper enquiry than I have been able to give them and that greater expertise than mine would prove the manuscript's provenance beyond doubt.

At present I can only say that I am as satisfied as I can be that the present narrative is a previously unknown work of Dr Watson, recording a previously unknown case of the world's greatest consulting detective, Sherlock Holmes.

Barrie Roberts, Walsall

One

The King's Governess

Despite the astonishing successes which my friend, Mr Sherlock Holmes, frequently had in the most abstruse enquiries, he was never willing to exploit his results to extend his clientele. From the very early days of his practice he was content to let word of his profession and his grasp of it spread slowly by word of mouth.

'I am well aware, Watson, that I might make myself available to the popular press or publish a small volume of my cases and thereby expose myself to a veritable deluge of enquiries, the greater part of which would be of no interest and many of which would have been invented so that some mindless timewaster might meet me face to face and forever after claim my acquaintance. No, I prefer that those who understand the importance of scientific detection should be aware of me and should recommend me where my skills, such as they are, may be put to useful purposes.'

He was in this mood one morning in the summer of 1897, when Mrs Hudson informed us that there was a lady below who had been recommended to call on him by the manager of an hotel.

'It seems she has been followed about by strangers since she came to London,' explained our landlady.

'And these persons who follow her,' said Holmes, 'no doubt they are swarthy persons who appear to be foreign and may have fearsome beards and moustaches? Is that so?'

'Why, that's exactly what she told me, Mr Holmes!' Mrs Hudson exclaimed.

'It was no great feat of deduction, Mrs Hudson. Every other

lady from the country or the provinces who sets foot in the capital rapidly begins to believe that she is being followed about by strange foreigners intent on doing her harm. It is, I regret to say, one of the common fancies of your sex, whereas if any such thing is taking place it will prove to be the activities of Cockney oglers.'

Mrs Hudson's features tightened. 'The lady is not from the country or the provinces,' she said. 'I believe that she is an American and she tells me that she is in London to meet with one of the guests who is coming for the Jubilee.'

'A visitor to Britain!' I exclaimed. 'Surely it would not hurt to give her the benefit of the doubt, Holmes?'

He eyed me, fishily. 'Your gallantry does you credit, Watson, if it is not the understandable desire of a widower to meet a new female. However, I confess that a visitor from America who has crossed the Atlantic to meet some royal personage in London might offer a little more interest than I had at first suspected. You may show her up, and please bring us some Ceylon tea, Mrs Hudson.'

He scrutinized the visiting card which Mrs Hudson had handed him while we awaited our caller.

'Mrs Diana Fordeland,' he read out. 'The name has a vaguely familiar ring, and it smacks of invention. Are we about to meet what is commonly called "an adventuress", Watson?'

A moment later Mrs Hudson brought in our guest. She was an upright lady in her middle years, who would once have been very pretty despite a rather prominent nose. Holmes showed her to the basket chair and introduced us.

Mrs Fordeland settled herself in the chair and drew off her gloves. 'You are very kind to see me with no notice, Mr Holmes,' she said.

'Ah!' exclaimed my friend. 'Forgive me, Mrs Fordeland. My housekeeper had surmised, wrongly, that you are American, however, you are, I believe, British. You are of Welsh ancestry, have lived in the Far East and now reside somewhere in the Eastern Provinces of Canada.'

Our visitor's eyes opened wide and her mouth tightened for an instant. 'You seem to know a great deal about me, Mr Holmes!'

4

'Not at all,' he said. 'I was merely considering the elements that became apparent when you spoke. Beyond that I can tell you only that you are a teacher, most probably of art, although I do not rule out other subjects.'

She laughed. 'That is really remarkable!' she exclaimed. 'You are entirely accurate. How do you do it? It cannot all be by my accent.'

Holmes smiled. 'It is only a matter of observation, madam. You carry yourself with dignity and have an air of one who is used to command. Among men that is commonplace and might indicate a military or naval officer, an important functionary in trade or industry or someone in the public service. These areas are still, alas, largely closed to your sex, and most of the employments available to women are of a subservient nature, except teaching. As to your artistic leanings, you dress in modest grey but wear finely crafted and unusual earrings and a brooch the unconventional placing of which lights your entire costume. You must surely be a person of artistic perception.'

She laughed again. 'Wonderful!' she said. 'I am of Welsh parentage; I have lived in India and the Far East, and I was, for some years, governess to the children of the late King of Mongkuria.'

The penny dropped. 'Of course!' I exclaimed. 'You wrote a book – two books. You wrote about your time in Mongkuria and you wrote a novel. I apologize. I should have recognized the name.'

She smiled and inclined her head gracefully. 'Why, thank you, Doctor. After the death of my husband it became necessary for me to support myself and my two children. That was what took me to Mongkuria and, when my time there ended, I had to fall back upon my only other talent and take to writing. Apart from the two books, I have written various articles for American magazines.'

'And what,' asked Holmes, 'brings you to London now?'

'A combination of purposes, Mr Holmes. I am on my way to Europe with my granddaughter, but it seemed an excellent opportunity to witness Her Majesty's Diamond Jubilee and to renew my acquaintance with King Chula of Mongkuria, who will be here for the ceremony. I had the honour of teaching His Highness when he was a boy.'

'How long have you been here?' asked my friend.

'We arrived five days ago. Since then we have occupied our time in making contact with old friends and relations and seeing the sights.'

'And you have been bothered – perhaps harassed?' enquired Holmes.

Mrs Fordeland frowned slightly and paused before replying. 'I think that "harassment" is probably too strong a word, but we have certainly been bothered.'

'In what way?' said Holmes.

'Initially,' she said, 'it was merely the observation that, wherever my granddaughter and I might be in London, we noted a small number of strange persons, apparently foreign. Now, I am aware,' she went on hastily, 'that the city at present is crowded with foreign visitors for the Jubilee and that there are many contingents of troops from all over the Empire camped in the parks, but these persons seemed to fit into no category of visitor or soldier that we recognized. Wherever we have been, at the Tower of London, in the zoological gardens, at Kew, one or more of these persons has been present in our immediate vicinity. At first we thought it merely a coincidence, but yesterday's events made it clear to me that there is some purpose in their presence. That was when I decided to take advice, and the manager of our hotel was kind enough to recommend you.'

There was a tap at the door, and our conversation paused while Mrs Hudson served tea. When we all had a cup Holmes leaned forward in his chair.

'You have referred to these people in the plural. How many of them are there?'

'There seem to be four, or perhaps five. Certainly no more than six. It is a little difficult to be sure, because we may not have been aware of all of them and because they seem to be in two separate groups.'

'Can you describe any of them?' asked Holmes.

'I hope that I may do better than that, Mr Holmes,' said the lady, and slipped a hand into her bag. 'I have not taught

6

drawing and painting for years without, I hope, learning something of visual observation. In the hope that these would assist you, I prepared them last night.'

She passed to my friend a small roll of papers which she had taken from her bag. Holmes unrolled them and examined them silently for a while. At last he looked up and said, 'They are very expertly drawn, Mrs Fordeland. Do you believe that they are good likenesses?'

'I hope so,' she said, apparently unruffled by his question. 'I flatter myself that I have an artist's eye and memory and my granddaughter agrees that the sketches resemble the principal four.'

Holmes passed the drawings to me and I could see at once that they fell into two pairs. Two of the four portraits showed lean men in their thirties, both with military moustaches. The third man possessed coarser features and a thick beard and moustache, giving him a distinctly foreign appearance. The fourth portrait was of a woman of some thirty years, but prematurely aged and with a face drawn by worry.

'You mentioned events yesterday which convinced you that you were the target of these persons' attention,' said Holmes. 'May I ask what happened?'

'We were travelling to visit an old friend who lives in Sussex. When we arrived at Waterloo Station in the morning, I noticed the two men with the military appearance loitering about the ticket office. Subsequently they caught the same train as us to Petersfield. That might have been coincidence, they may perhaps have been visitors to Britain like ourselves, but at Petersfield we changed trains. We boarded a local train, a stopping train to Midhurst in Sussex, as my friend lives in a village along that line. It was at Petersfield Station, on our return journey, that I was able to confirm that we are being followed, Mr Holmes.'

'In what way?' he asked.

'The Midhurst train pulled into a small siding at Petersfield. As I left the little platform, my granddaughter was behind me and I turned to speak to her. As I did so, I saw the two military men alight from the train, followed at a distance by the other couple. Now, I am just about prepared to accept that the presence of one pair on the train from London to Petersfield was a coincidence, but the appearance of both alighting from that little local train at the same time that my granddaughter and I arrived in Petersfield is, I believe, reasonable confirmation that these four people are following us.'

Holmes nodded slowly, then steepled his long fingers and bent over them. 'Coincidence,' he said, 'is far too often put forward as an explanation, and frequently extended beyond the bounds of credibility. I entirely accept that you are being followed. Now we must discover why.'

He looked up suddenly. 'Can you think,' he said, 'of any reason why these people are so interested in your movements?'

The lady appeared to think for a moment then shook her head firmly. 'No,' she said, 'I cannot. Do you believe that they mean my granddaughter or me some harm, Mr Holmes?'

He shook his head. 'I think not,' he replied. 'The most obvious forms of harm would be robbery, kidnapping or murder, and it would seem that they have had ample opportunity to commit these, which they have not taken. You are convinced that the two pairs are separate?'

'Absolutely,' she said. 'Apart from the fact that I have never seen all four together, the bearded man and his companion seem positively to avoid the other two. In addition, there is a distinct difference in their dress.'

'In their dress?' queried Holmes.

'Yes,' she said. 'The two men seem to be men of business in some degree, they dress well but discreetly. The bearded man and his consort are very different. Their dress can sometimes be almost bizarre, and always appears to have been assembled from second-hand items. For example, on the platform at Petersfield the bearded man was wearing a rather faded cricket blazer, which had once shown loud stripes, with a bowler hat.'

'Good heavens!' I exclaimed. 'A striped blazer and a bowler hat?'

'Indeed,' said Mrs Fordeland. 'Sometimes I believe that the bearded man is trying to make himself obvious to me.'

'It is certainly not a discreet disguise,' agreed Holmes. He uncoiled himself from his chair and stood up.

'Mrs Fordeland,' he said, 'I am certain that you and your granddaughter are in no immediate danger, but you were quite right to bring the matter to me. There is much here that requires investigation. I shall commence my researches and, in the meantime, I recommend that you go about your business. If, however, you observe any change in the behaviour of your followers – any change at all – please communicate with me at once.'

Mrs Fordeland and I rose and she moved towards the door. 'Thank you, Mr Holmes,' she said. 'It is a great comfort to me to have your observations and to know that you are looking into the problem. You may be assured that I shall let you know of any change.'

We took our farewells and, when the door had closed behind our client, Holmes resumed his seat.

'What do you make of it all, Holmes?' I asked.

'It is a singular affair, Watson. It reminds me a little of that curious game of "Grandmother's Footsteps" which took place in the Tumblety affair ten years ago,* but I am also moved to wonder what connection the lady has with Russia.'

'With Russia?' I said, and I had barely spoken the words when I heard footsteps on the stairs and the swish of a dress. There was a quick tap at the door and our client reappeared.

'They are here now, Mr Holmes,' she said breathlessly. 'One of them was outside when I reached the pavement!'

*See *Sherlock Holmes and the Royal Flush* by Barrie Roberts.

Two

The Bear's Spoor

Holmes stepped quickly to the window, glanced down into the street, then sprang for the door.

'Stay with Watson!' he commanded our client and plunged out. We heard him taking the steps three at a time and I looked from the window in time to see him emerge on to the pavement and look about him.

I could see nobody who matched any of Mrs Fordeland's sketches, but I did not know whether Holmes had a better view from the street. Certainly he turned suddenly southward and strode off briskly. I returned to my chair and summoned Mrs Hudson to bring us some more tea.

'I hope,' said our visitor, after we had been served, 'that I have not involved Mr Holmes in any danger.'

'Think nothing of it, dear lady,' I assured her. 'Sherlock Holmes has never allowed danger to deter him from an enquiry and, in any case, he is peculiarly well equipped to deal with most ordinary dangers. Apart from being a bare-knuckle fighter of professional standard and a skilled swordsman, he is also an exponent of the Japanese fighting technique known as *baritsu*. I do not think you need fear for his safety.'

'I am glad to hear you say it,' she said. 'I have seen baritsu demonstrated while I was living in Singapore. I thought it rather similar to Cornish wrestling. In Mongkuria they employ most unusual methods of personal combat, frequently involving their bare feet. I confess that, when I first arrived in the Kingdom and witnessed boys practising their skills, I thought it barbaric and the use of the foot very un-British, but I came to realize that it is, in fact, a very skilful affair and can look

10

remarkably graceful, far more so than a bare-knuckle bout, where men are battered until their hearts fail, or even a fight under the Queensberry Rules which permit beating an opponent into unconsciousness. By comparison, the Mongkurian manner seems more civilized.'

The door opened and Sherlock Holmes rejoined us. 'If that tea is still warm, Watson, I should welcome a cup,' he said, as he dropped into a chair.

Mrs Fordeland watched him expectantly as he took a long draught of tea, until he turned to her.

'You have told us,' he said, 'that you have lived in India and Mongkuria and Canada. Have you been in other parts of the world?'

'Many,' she said. 'I was born in India, I have been in Malaya. Mongkuria you know about. I have lived briefly in England and in Ireland, in Australia and the United States of America, and in Canada. Why do you ask, Mr Holmes?'

He looked thoughtful. You cannot identify any present reason why these four pursuers should be interested in your movements, Mrs Fordeland. Therefore it seems likely that their concern is with something in your past. Now, they are evidently not Indian, Malayan or Mongkurian, from their colouring and from the fact that they lack the distinctively handsome features of the Mongkurian people. If they were Canadian or American, I would have expected their interest in you to have shown itself in the vicinity of your home. Have you experienced anything of the kind at home?'

'No,' she said. 'Halifax is a great port, and there are strangers from all over the world walking its streets, but I'm sure I should have noticed anything like the persistent following that has gone on here in London.'

Holmes picked up the four sketches from his desk and looked at them for some time in silence. At last he said, 'You did not mention having been in Russia.'

For a moment his client seemed flustered, but it was only a moment. 'True,' she agreed, 'but you asked where I have lived. I have not lived in Russia, though I have travelled the whole length of the country.'

'Surely not for pleasure?' Holmes suggested.

11

'No, no, Mr Holmes, though much of my journey was pleasurable. On the death of the King of Mongkuria, the Regency Council did not renew my contract as governess to the royal children. I had relatively small means and was forced to support my two children and myself by my pen. My writing met with success in the United States and the magazine *Young Women of America* commissioned a series of articles from Russia. For that reason I travelled, as I said, the entire length of that vast country. I believe that I am,' she concluded, with pardonable pride, 'the first and only western woman to have done so.'

'And what,' asked Holmes, 'did you make of Russia?'

'It is an extraordinary country,' she said. 'Not only in its vast size, its huge distances, its great variations of climate, but in the contrasts in society. In Moscow and Saint Petersburg, in their great cities, one may see art and drama the equal of any in the world, and meet a society that equals anything in London, Paris, Vienna, New York or where you will; yet, in the countryside, no distance from those great cities, one can see a life that seems infinitely worse than the life of English serfs in the Middle Ages. The Russian aristocracy are all that the French were and worse, and I suspect that they will go the same way.'

'You did not express these views in Russia, or in your articles?' asked Holmes.

'Certainly not, Mr Holmes. Whatever I thought of the wretchedness and oppression that I witnessed, I kept my mouth shut, though it was difficult on occasion. It seemed to me that my usefulness would be in making these things more widely known outside Russia.'

'So you did describe them in your articles?'

'Of course,' she replied, 'but if you are about to suggest that something which I wrote in those articles has upset someone in Russia, then I have to point out that it was nearly twenty years ago and that I did not identify people by their real names. It would have to be someone with exaggerated sensitivity and an extremely long memory who would concern himself with anything I wrote then.'

Holmes nodded. 'Very true,' he agreed. 'Nevertheless, there is a clear Russian element in this affair.'

'Why do you say so?' the lady asked.

Holmes picked up the sheaf of drawings from his desk. 'When I first saw your sketches I believed that I knew the identity of one of your followers. Now that I have seen how accurately you recalled and drew the bearded man, I have no doubt that the others are as accurate. I am now sure of the identity of this man.'

He selected one of the drawings and tapped it with his fore-finger. 'That,' he said, 'is a portrait of Major Ivan Kyriloff, who is a military attaché at the Russian Embassy.'

Our client looked puzzled. 'Why on earth should such a man take an interest in my trips about London, Mr Holmes?'

'Why indeed?' said Holmes. 'Furthermore, although Major Kyriloff passes as a military attaché, that is not his real duty. You may not be aware – few people are – that the Tzar has many more agents in the East End of London than the Metropolitan Police. They are there to watch over and to infiltrate if possible the bands of refugees from Russia who settle there, more than a few of whom are possessed of a desire to overthrow their former master. Major Kyriloff's duty is to organize and oversee these spies, informers, agents provocateurs and saboteurs. He does not normally pursue his own quarry, he has far too many agents. That he has chosen, or been forced, to do so in your case, Mrs Fordeland, implies that Major Kyriloff or one of his superiors regards something about you as vital to the interests of the Tzar.'

'I accept your reasoning, Mr Holmes, but I cannot fathom why I should be of interest to the Tzar or his minions in London,' said our guest. 'I have told you, it was nearly twenty years ago that I was in Russia. Why have they not followed me in America or in Canada if they believe me in some way important?'

'That,' said my friend, 'is one of the several mysteries which surround this matter. The Tzar's intelligence service reaches deep into the heart of the United States and the British Empire. If you are of interest because of some connection with your Russian travels or the articles arising from it, then it would have been easy to track you down in America or Canada, but they have not done so. It seems that it is your presence in London that draws their interest.'

He lit a cigarette and smoked for a few minutes, gazing thoughtfully out of the window.

'Tell me,' he said, swivelling suddenly back to our client, 'have you made any secret of the reasons why you are in London?'

The lady smiled. 'Heavens no!' she exclaimed. 'Quite the opposite. One or two newspapers have carried items recalling that I was the English governess to the King of Mongkuria and wrote a book about it, and they have said that I am here to see the Jubilee ceremonies and to meet with King Chula.'

'And King Chula's country is of little interest to Russia,' said Holmes. 'It might well interest France or Holland, and the King's invitation to the Diamond Jubilee is evidence of our own interest in his sphere, but I cannot imagine that the Russians have any realistic interest in that region. Nevertheless, of one thing I am certain, Mrs Fordeland, and that is that both pairs of your pursuers are Russian.'

'Both pairs?' repeated our client. 'Do you then recognize either of the second pair?'

He shook his head. 'No,' he said. 'The woman seems to have Slavic features, but the man's face is so concealed by his whiskers that it is difficult to tell.'

'I had thought while I was trying to draw him that his face, insofar as one can see it, seemed Russian, but perhaps it was a slight resemblance to an interpreter I met in Russia. But you are certain, Mr Holmes?'

'That the man is Russian? Yes,' he said.

My friend slipped his fingers into his coat pocket and drew out a twist of paper.

'When I ran into the street,' he said, 'your watcher had dropped his cigarette and started to make off towards the cab rank by Tussauds. The hot weather and the Jubilee visitors to London meant that there was a shortage of cabs and he was able to make good his escape from me by taking the only vehicle on the rank. At that point I abandoned my pursuit and returned here, but I paused to recover the remains of his cigarette.'

He unrolled the twist of paper and revealed that it contained a cigarette end and a little heap of ash, which he carefully shook out on to a sheet of white paper.

'Expertise in the varieties of tobacco is a subject that is stupidly ignored by many professional detectives,' he commented. 'Watson will tell you that I have published a small text on the subject.' He spread the ash with his fore-finger and took his lens from his pocket. 'As I suspected,' he said, as he examined the ash with the lens, 'this is a coarse mixture of a dark Russian tobacco and a more mellow Turkish. That alone is not enough for our purposes, but this, I think, makes my case.'

He used his thumbnail to split the cigarette end's paper. It revealed not tobacco, but a crude tube made from a piece of card. Holmes straightened it with his fingers.

'The card is merely a piece of an advertisement,' he said, 'and is unimportant. Its significance lies in its application. Whoever made this cigarette – and I think we may reason-ably infer that it was your bearded follower – inserted the cardboard tube to cool the strong tobacco. That is a Russian practice. Evidently he can purchase suitable tobaccos in Britain, but not the Russian cigarettes which include such a tube.'

'It establishes,' he continued, 'beyond reasonable doubt, that both pairs of watchers are Russians. The first pair, we know, come from the Russian Embassy. This second pair seem more like the Russian Socialists who gather in the East End. The presence of Major Kyriloff and such a pair implies Russian political affairs, but you have said nothing which suggests any such involvement, Mrs Fordeland.'

'Nor is there!' she exclaimed. 'Even while I was in that country I observed the proprieties of my status as a reporter and did not intervene in their politics. It is true that I have certain sympathies for some ideals of the Socialists and Anarchists who oppose the Tzar's tyranny, but I detest their habits of bomb-throwing and assassination. You may be assured, Mr Holmes, that whatever this is all about has nothing to do with Russian politics.'

Sherlock Holmes nodded, thoughtfully. 'So,' he said, 'we have identified two agents of the Tzar and, possibly, two of his opponents. My brother Mycroft has connections with those whose business it is to know what Major Kyriloff is up to, and I shall ask his assistance. As to the other two, since we cannot identify them, we must strive to do so, and I believe that is best done by setting a simple trap.'

Three

Holmes Sets a Trap

One of the most astonishing abilities of my friend Sherlock Holmes was the capacity to predict the future course of events with remarkable accuracy, having drawn inferences from facts and indications that others, including myself, had ignored. Nevertheless, in the matter of Mrs Fordeland's followers he was, I believe, nonplussed by the outcome of his plan to identify the bearded man and his companion.

The 'trap' was, in itself, perfectly reasonable and simple. On the morning following our first meeting with our client, she was to leave her granddaughter with friends and take a cab to Baker Street. Her retinue of watchers would, inevitably, assume that she was taking a second consultation with Holmes, but that was not so.

On her arrival at our rooms, I was awaiting the lady, but Holmes was not. My friend, clad in one of his impenetrable disguises, was already seated in a closed cab a little distance along the street.

Mrs Fordeland assured me that, as her cab had turned into Baker Street, the following vehicle, carrying Major Kyriloff and his colleague, had dropped back. They had evidently drawn the expected conclusion and were most probably lying in wait at the bottom of the street.

A second cab brought the other two Russians. The bearded man alighted in Baker Street and took up a position across the street from 221b, where he loitered and rolled a cigarette.

Mrs Fordeland and I took a cup of tea and chatted, for long enough to give our watcher across the street confirmation that another consultation with Holmes was taking place. When we believed that a sufficient time had passed, we left together and I escorted the lady to the cab rank by Tussauds.

The ruse worked admirably. Our bearded follower fell in behind and, when we took a cab, jumped into one which had been waiting, and Mrs Fordeland and I set out for her hotel with both pairs of Russians following us at a discreet distance and Holmes following the second pair.

Arrived at the lady's hotel, a discreet glance from the window assured us that, while Major Kyriloff's colleague was still maintaining a position outside, the bearded man and his companion had taken their cab away, followed, I had no doubt, by Sherlock Holmes.

I had expected that my friend would follow the watchers to their lair and return fairly shortly, to report that they were denizens of one of those East End boarding houses which were, at that time, often full of refugees from and plotters against the Tzar's regime. Rather to my surprise, Holmes was gone for much of the day.

As we awaited his return, the lady and I took luncheon together, during which she regaled me with many amusing and extraordinary anecdotes culled from her years of travel in the East and in Australia, America and Canada. As I expected, from reading her books some years earlier, she was an accomplished narrator, with an observant eye, a good memory and a strong sense of humour, so that our meal and much of the afternoon passed very pleasantly.

So it was that it was tea time before I began seriously to wonder at my friend's absence. Mrs Fordeland expressed concern that the persons he had followed might have seen through his disguise and waylaid him. I was able to assure her that Sherlock Holmes disguised was totally unrecognizable and that he was well provided against harm by the extreme quickness of his wits, his training in bare-knuckle fighting and his ability in swordplay and baritsu. I diverted her fears with a number of anecdotes of occasions when Holmes' disguises had proved impenetrable even to me.

We were taking our tea in the hotel's conservatory when a waiter approached and told Mrs Fordeland that there was a clergyman in the lobby asking for her and saying that he had a message for her.

'Be careful!' I warned her. 'This may be some ruse of the watchers.'

She nodded, but bade the waiter show the man in to us. I eased my chair a little away from the table and grasped my Adams revolver, which I had not neglected to slip into my coat pocket that morning.

The waiter returned accompanied by a figure who seemed, at first sight, completely harmless. The clergyman was an elderly, stooped individual, in shabby black and carrying a bundle of tracts. He peered about him through thick, half-round spectacles and introduced himself in a reedy, elderly voice as a missionary in the East End.

Despite my warning, Mrs Fordeland ushered our visitor into a chair and pressed upon him a cup of tea and a selection of cakes. Tea he accepted, but he insisted that he must follow the abstemious example of his Master and take only bread and butter.

I waited in growing impatience as he supped his tea and munched steadily at two slices of bread and butter. When he had done, he gazed about him again, as though surprised to find himself there, then took out a slim black notebook from an inside pocket.

'I have a message,' he said, 'which I have been asked to deliver to a Mrs Fordeland at this hotel.'

'A message?' I said. 'From whom?'

'You must not rush me, Doctor,' he said. 'I am an old man and the memory is not as useful now as once it was. I have been today in the vicinity of Commercial Road, attempting, as always, to bring a little light into the harsh world of the foreigners there. In the course of my efforts I was approached by a young man who seemed to be some kind of salesman. He made a generous contribution to my mission on the understanding that I would deliver his message when I returned to town.'

He raised his notebook as though to peer at the pages, but his eyes dilated and he stared past us at the conservatory windows beyond.

19

'Great Heavens!' he exclaimed.

Mrs Fordeland and I swung our heads in unison. There was nothing untoward that I could see beyond the panes. The hotel's small garden lay in the sunlight and nobody was in sight.

When we turned back the lined features and spectacles of the old cleric had disappeared. Above the shabby black clothing were the familiar features of Sherlock Holmes. Mrs Fordeland stared for a moment, then emitted a loud laugh. I shook my head slowly.

'Holmes,' I said. 'Why do I never realize that it is you?'

He laughed. 'I always think it a pity that many of my best dramatic creations are wasted upon an audience which will never know that it was witnessing a performance. It is some small consolation to have your applause, Watson. Now, Mrs Fordeland, if I may rescind my former refusal of cake and take another cup of tea, I shall be able to report to you the result of today's enquiries.'

Once fully refreshed he leaned back in his chair.

'When you both arrived here this morning,' he began, 'Major Kyriloff left his aide to watch the hotel and took himself off. The other two watchers seemed to be satisfied that they need not watch further and their cab drove off, followed at a reasonable distance by my own conveyance.

'I had expected,' he went on, 'that they would make for an Underground station and travel to the East End, or perhaps take their cab all the way. I admit to being a little surprised when they took their cab to Victoria and boarded a train to Sussex. I followed, of course, and found that their destination was the village of Burriwell, under the Downs.'

He paused and sipped his tea. 'It is a dangerous practice to believe that, because the majority of a class of people behave in a particular fashion, that all persons of that type will so behave. It is misleading to convince oneself that all Frenchmen are romantics, all Jews financially acute, all Irishmen aggressive or all Scots careful with their money, and I fear that I had fallen into that error. I had identified the bearded gentleman and his companion as Russian refugees, and so unconsciously expected them to be located in the eastern slums among their compatriots.'

'I was therefore,' he continued, 'the more surprised to find that, not only are our mysterious pair living in a pretty village by the Sussex Downs, they are dwelling, not in some rented cottage, but as house guests of a wealthy maiden lady.'

Both Mrs Fordeland and I were surprised by Holmes' information, but his next remark was an even greater surprise to me.

'Tell me, Mrs Fordeland,' he said, 'does the name Agatha Wortley-Swan mean anything to you?'

Our client looked completely perplexed. 'No,' she said. 'I am quite sure that I have never heard that name before.'

'I have,' I said.

Holmes turned. 'You know the lady's name, Watson? In what connection, pray?'

'When I was finishing my degree in London, some twenty years ago or more, and when I was at Netley for the Army medical certificate, Agatha Wortley-Swan was a well-known society beauty. Her picture appeared in the *Graphic* and the *Illustrated London* more than once, and I believe some of the fellows at Netley actually knew the lady.'

'Excellent!' exclaimed Holmes, 'but she has never married, and my researches in the village and my gossipy enquiries in the village inn have referred me only to some unspecified "tragedy" which left the lady single. Do you recall that, Watson?'

I cast my memory back two decades. 'She was engaged,' I remembered, 'because all the fellows at Netley were heartbroken, but it went wrong. Her fiancé died, I believe, in peculiar circumstances. I think, perhaps, that he was murdered.'

'Murdered!' repeated Holmes, and his eyes lit with that peculiar sparkle which appeared when his mind was fully and enthusiastically engaged. 'Do you, by any chance, remember the luckless fiancé's name?'

I sifted my memory again. 'I think,' I said, 'that he was a Captain Parkes of the Royal West Mallows.'

Holmes snapped his fingers. 'Of course!' he exclaimed.

He rose abruptly. 'We must take our leave, Mrs Fordeland. My device today has given me more data and, with the help of Watson's memory for a pretty face, I hope soon to have yet more. Rest assured that we are on the way to identifying this mysterious pair and finding out the nature of their interest in you. In the meantime, do not forget to keep me aware of any change in the patterns of their behaviour.'

Holmes was silent on the way back to Baker Street, drumming his fingers impatiently on the handle of his stick and staring fixedly ahead of him. At our door he sprang from the cab and raced upstairs. By the time I had paid the cabby and followed him, he was sunk in an armchair leafing rapidly through one of the large scrapbooks into which he entered items which he deemed might be of use in the future.

'Parkes, was it, Watson? Was he not murdered in Paris?'

'It's a long time, Holmes. I believe that he was murdered abroad, but I would not swear that it was Paris.'

He continued flicking rapidly through the pages, then gave a cry of triumph. 'I have it, Watson! Listen to this!' and he read me the entry.

'From our correspondent in Paris. The large English community in this city has been stunned by the discovery of the fate of the missing Captain Parkes. Readers of our earlier notices of the matter will recall that Captain Parkes has been missing for some five days. The French authorities now inform us that a body taken from the River Seine has been identified by a brother officer as that of Captain Parkes. It appears that Captain Parkes, who went missing after attending a diplomatic reception with his fiancée, the noted beauty Miss Agatha Wortley-Swan, escorted the lady to her hotel and, on his way home, had the misfortune to fall in with some of the boulevard thieves who so plague this city. Perhaps the gallant officer attempted to defend himself too fiercely, because a source in the City's police informs us that he had been severely beaten by a number of persons before being stabbed. This information is confirmed by Captain Wilmshaw, a brother officer, whose unhappy task it was to identify his friend's remains.'

He closed the book with a snap and rose to replace it on the shelf.

'But what happened?' I asked. 'Did they never find the killers?'

'No, indeed,' replied Holmes. 'That is why I have Captain Parkes' death indexed under U, for "unsolved". The Paris police, it appears, were content to lay the matter to the charge of some unidentified boulevard robber and take no further steps.'

'But what has all this to do with Mrs Fordeland?' I protested.

'Now there, Watson, you put your finger on exactly the right point. What, indeed, is the connection?'

Four

The Bear's Whisper

On the next morning I rose to find that the atmosphere in our sitting room at Baker Street was thick with the stale smoke of Holmes' pipe. He himself was sitting immobile, perched on top of a pile of cushions upon the sofa. His face was set in an expression of grim concentration and his eyes half-closed. As I pulled back the curtains and slid up the windows he barely acknowledged my 'Good morning.'

It was only when I had been seated for some minutes that he took his pipe from his mouth, opened his eyes and looked at me.

'It does not make any manner of sense, Watson,' he said, and I realized that it was the case of Mrs Fordeland to which he referred. 'I have spent the night examining the facts from every angle, and it does not make sense!'

He uncoiled himself from the sofa, knocked out his pipe in the fireplace and sat at the table, just as Mrs Hudson arrived to serve breakfast. He was silent over our meal, eating only a little toast and drinking several cups of coffee.

When the meal had been cleared away he remained at the table, gazing out of the window and drumming his long fingers on the tablecloth.

'We have insufficient data, Watson,' he declared at last. 'All that we have learned appears to be true, yet none of it is capable of being connected in any meaningful fashion. *Ergo*, there must be a missing piece or pieces.'

'How do you propose to obtain new data?' I asked. 'Mrs Fordeland appears to have told us all that she knows of the matter. Where else can you enquire?'

'There is my brother,' he said. 'The unresolved death of Captain Parkes in Paris will have given rise to representations between the two governments. Mycroft's department will have been involved. Somewhere in their voluminous files there may well be some small piece of information which will put us on the right track.'

'Shall you go to his club?' I asked.

He shook his head. 'Oh no. The matter may be urgent. As we do not know the purposes of the Russians in following our client, we cannot be sure that she is not in any danger.'

'But I thought you assured her that there was no danger,' I said.

'I pointed out to Mrs Fordeland that, if her followers wished her immediate harm, they would have done it before now. I still believe that to be true, but I do not discount the possibility that some factor in this situation which we do not understand may change and place her or her granddaughter in danger. We will act speedily. Be so kind as to ring for our boots, Watson.'

Within minutes we were in a cab, bound for the great building which housed the department of government for which Mycroft Holmes worked.

I had known Sherlock Holmes for several years before he so much as mentioned to me that he had a brother. I recall that it was in connection with the 'Greek Interpreter' case that he finally introduced me to Mycroft. Before the introduction Holmes explained that his older brother was cleverer than he but physically lazy. He lived a curious existence, rotating between his bachelor chambers, his office and the strange club called the Diogenes Club (of which he was not only a member, but a founder). It was the absolute rule of the Diogenes Club that no member might speak to another on its premises.

Holmes also explained that his brother was so important a functionary of the government that there were occasions when he was, virtually, the British government. At the time I was inclined to regard this as an exaggeration, but in my observation of Mycroft Holmes over the ensuing decade I came to realize that he really was at least as intelligent as his younger brother and that the power he wielded in government circles seemed to have no bounds.

25

We were soon at the great Italianate building that housed Mycroft's department, and were quickly led up a magnificent staircase to his office. When we were shown into his room, Mycroft sat behind a large and ornate desk, in front of tall windows that looked down upon the treetops of the park.

He rose at our entry and showed us to chairs. 'Sherlock, Doctor,' he said, 'this is a surprise. I was thinking that I must drop you a note.'

'Really?' said Holmes. 'Is there some little matter in which I can assist your office?'

Mycroft shook his head. 'Oh no,' he said, 'but it seems that you have been upsetting our Russian allies.'

'If that is news to you, Mycroft, it is also to me. In what way have I caused upset and how does the matter come to your ears?'

'You know me, Sherlock,' said his brother. 'Usually I am bored to distraction by the diplomatic social round, but there are occasions when one must suffer for one's country. There were, I am afraid, sufficient reasons of policy for me to make an appearance last evening at a reception at the Russian Embassy.'

'You mean you wished to listen to indiscreet conversations once the vodka was flowing,' remarked Holmes. 'Pray continue.'

'Something along those lines,' said Mycroft. 'It was supposed to be an event to introduce the Russians who are here for Her Majesty's Jubilee, so every other person was a cousin of the Tzar. Your old sparring partner Major Kyriloff was there, hanging about an offensive fellow called Count Stepan Skovinski-Rimkoff. Kyriloff introduced us, making a great point that Rimkoff is yet another cousin of the Tzar and the fellow looks at me with a fishy eye and says, "Are you not the brother of Sherlock Holmes, the criminal agent?"'

'I do apologize, Mycroft, that you should be forced to own my kinship in public,' said Holmes.

'Not at all, brother, not at all. I was pleased to claim kinship with the man that Dr Watson has made famous. It was his next remark that caused me concern.'

'And what was that?' asked Holmes.

'He said, and I quote him verbatim, "I am familiar with his adventures through the stories in your *Strand Magazine*. I applaud his intelligence and courage, but unfortunately he sometimes involves himself in things which are not his concern." "Really?" I said. "Was there something in particular which you had in mind?" He gave me the fishy eye again and then said, "Your brother has chosen to interest himself in a matter which is of no criminal consequence whatsoever. However, it is an affair which touches upon the honour of my country. You would be well advised to suggest that he leaves the matter alone." With which he tossed off his vodka and marched off. Damned rude, I thought.'

Mycroft delved into a pocket of his coat and extracted a snuffbox and a large silk handkerchief.

'What do you know about Count Skovinski-Rimkoff?' asked Holmes.

'He's as rich as Croesus. Came into an enormous fortune when he was about twelve. He's in his late forties now and owns a chunk of Russia about the size of England and Wales. He's a cousin of the Tzar, but has a thoroughly unwholesome reputation.'

'Really?' said Holmes. 'In what way?'

'He was over here some years ago, in a private capacity. He got involved in a decidedly unpleasant affair with a gay young woman and almost caused a scandal. It seems that he paid the lady for some specialized service and became rather enthusiastic, so that she was quite severely injured. Everything was all being covered up very nicely by Kyriloff's agents when the young lady turns up at a police station with a solicitor in tow and demands a prosecution against the count. That was where Her Majesty's government got drawn into the thing. The Russian ambassador was applying pressure and trying to persuade us to jail the woman. I had to point out to him that this is not Holy Russia, that we do not arbitrarily imprison people who are an embarrassment. I suggested that a deal less threats and a moderately large sum of money might cure the problem.'

'And did it?'

'Oh yes. We never heard any more of the matter.'

'You don't think his remarks to you might refer to that incident?'

'I don't see how they could, unless you are seeking to reopen the whole sordid affair. You're not, are you?'

Holmes shook his head. 'This is the first time I've ever heard of the count,' he said.

'Well, you must let me tell you all of it, Sherlock. It wasn't just Count Rimkoff. I was still considering the fellow's rudeness,' he continued, applying a pinch of snuff to the back of his hand, 'when Kyriloff spots me and slides over. He came and stood beside me, all smiles, twiddling that little moustache of his, and he says, very quietly, so that no one around would hear, "I see you have been talking to Count Stepan." "I have been talked at by him," I said, and Kyriloff smiled that unpleasant and oleaginous smile of his. "Ah, Mycroft," he said, "Stepan is new to the diplomatic circuit. He does not wish anything to go wrong which might reflect upon Mother Russia. Nevertheless, you would be doing your brother a favour if you suggested to him that he drop the case." Before I could ask what case, he'd tipped me a nod and vanished into the crowd.'

He took his snuff, sighed luxuriously, then sneezed formidably into the handkerchief.

'What did you do?' asked Holmes, once his brother had settled again.

'What did I do?' Mycroft repeated. 'Why, I decided that I was not going to stand about in full diplomatic fig like an ornamental pillar box so that the Russian diplomatic service and its attendant spies could use me to send postcards to you, so I made my excuses and left.'

He was silent for a while, his watery grey eyes resting on his brother.

'I cannot avoid wondering, Sherlock,' he said after a while, 'what it is that you have been doing to upset this wretched Count Stepan and the appalling Kyriloff. It would be awkward if you were to do anything which caused a contretemps with Russia just at the time of Her Majesty's celebration. After all, she is related to the Romanoffs.'

'Since Her Majesty,' said Holmes with a faint smile, 'is

related to almost all of the crowned heads of Europe, I find it difficult to believe that her government guides its foreign policies entirely by a desire not to upset the royal cousins. Why does Count Rimkoff loom so large in matters diplomatic?'

'Oh, he is hardly a diplomat, Sherlock. No, no, he is one of those invited to the Jubilee ceremony and that gives him diplomatic importance. The process of inviting foreigners to such an event is a delicate one. Where the British colonies and territories are concerned there is no problem. An invitation is issued and the individual concerned brushes down his best uniform, jumps into a canoe, a rickshaw or a palanquin and makes for the nearest port, turning up at Westminster, spick and span, several weeks later. No problem at all. With foreigners it's a question of which ones we want to invite, who they want us to invite and who we're prepared to accept. It can be awfully sticky, you know. Now, this fellow's a cousin of the Tzar, so that makes it worse. You're not doing anything that might embarrass us, are you, Sherlock?'

'Really, brother,' said the younger Holmes, 'you should know that I am the last man who would willingly embarrass Her Majesty. You do me less than justice – after all, it was Watson and I who averted a serious plot against Her Majesty's Golden Jubilee, ten years ago, or had you forgotten?'*

'True, true,' agreed his brother, 'but you cannot blame me for worrying. You do have a certain habit of pursuing your enquiries without much consideration of their effects.'

'It would be of great assistance to me if you could indicate what it is that I am doing that so bothers Major Kyriloff and Count Rimkoff.'

Mycroft shook his head slowly. 'I have no idea, Sherlock. I have relayed to you faithfully the remarks that they made, but I do not pretend to understand them.'

'Then I shall have to bear your information in mind in trying to unravel my little problem and make sure that I do not disrupt affairs of state or the splendour of Her Majesty's ceremony. In the meantime, perhaps you will assist me with the enquiry which brought me here.'

* See *Sherlock Holmes and the Royal Flush* by Barrie Roberts.

'Certainly, if I can,' said Mycroft.

'I need your assistance in the matter of an unsolved murder,' said Holmes.

'An unsolved murder!' repeated his brother. 'Hardly my line of country, I think.'

Five

A Minor Incident

The elder Holmes brother extracted his snuffbox from his pocket and went through his previous performance while we waited. When he had replaced his box and the silk hanky in his pockets he looked up again.

'No, Sherlock,' he said, shaking his head. 'I do not think that I can help you with an unsolved murder. Much as I enjoy an intellectual challenge, I find them aplenty in the vagaries of politicians and rulers. Why you choose to seek yours among the criminal classes I have never understood. Murders are not the affair of this department. Surely your friends at Scotland Yard can assist?'

'There are no criminal classes, Mycroft. The vagaries, morals, ambitions and behaviour of politicians are precisely comparable with those of the meanest thief in Whitechapel, as no one knows better than you. As to my friends, as you call them, at the Yard, they will have had nothing to do with this matter, which is why I came to you. I am interested in the murder of a British citizen in Paris, some twenty years ago.'

Mycroft Holmes nodded slowly. 'Ah,' he said. 'I see. Yes, such a matter might become the business of this department if there were no speedy resolution by the French authorities. You say that the matter remains unresolved after twenty years?'

'That is my understanding,' said Holmes. 'I believe that the French police attributed the crime to the action of street robbers and have made no serious effort to close the case. Does your office have a file on the affair?'

'Sadly there are often occasions when our citizens become

31

the victims of murderers overseas, but it is rarely that such incidents fall within the responsibilities of this department. Have you any details?'

'I know only what appeared in the English press at the time,' said Holmes. 'The victim was a British Army officer, one Captain Parkes. It seems that he had attended some public function with his fiancée, Miss Agatha Wortley-Swan, and escorted her home afterwards. At some time after delivering the lady to her abode, Captain Parkes disappeared. His body was taken from the Seine some days later and the French police expressed the view that he had been set upon by street bandits.'

Mycroft pursed his lips reflectively. 'Agatha Wortley-Swan,' he said. 'I recall that young lady, and now that you mention her, I do recollect that we were involved in dealings with the French. The lady's father was a wealthy manufacturer and he brought a deal of pressure to bear when the case was not solved. What is it that you require, Sherlock?'

'If a file still exists,' said Holmes, 'I would welcome a sight of it.'

Mycroft Holmes pursed his lips again. 'I am sure that a file still exists,' he said. 'We seem to have an inflexible rule against throwing away any piece of paper, which makes it all the more important that we guard carefully the documents which we accumulate. I am not at all sure that even I have the authority to let you see such a file.'

'Tush, Mycroft,' ejaculated Holmes. 'If you are worried that I may come to learn the lengths to which Her Majesty's government will go when pressed by a wealthy manufacturer, you need not be alarmed. I am solely concerned with learning whatever I can about the circumstances of Captain Parkes' death and the investigation.'

'Perhaps it would help,' suggested his brother, 'if you were to explain your interest in the affair.'

With his customary succinctness, Holmes told the story, omitting no consequential detail from the moment when Mrs Fordeland first appeared at Baker Street. Mycroft heard him out in silence.

'What do you make,' he asked, after Holmes' narrative ended, 'of the personal involvement of Major Kyriloff?'

'For Kyriloff to give this matter his personal attention and involvement indicates to me that the presence of Mrs Fordeland in London is perceived by him, or by someone who can order his actions, as in some way a threat to Russian interests. What you tell me of the remarks by Kyriloff and Count Rimkoff merely strengthens that belief.'

'And what,' asked Mycroft, 'do you believe is their interest in the lady?'

'They follow her about openly, as though they wish her to be aware of them, yet they take no step to interfere with her movements. It would appear that they suspect or fear some action that she may take or some person she may contact, but they are not sufficiently sure of themselves to move to prevent her.'

'Have you any idea what that action or contact may be, Sherlock?'

Holmes shook his head. 'The most frustrating aspect of the whole affair is my complete inability to make a sensible connection between the Russians – either pair of them – and my client.'

'Yet you say she was once in Russia,' reflected Mycroft.

'But that was more than a quarter of a century ago. Her articles have been long published and forgotten. If it were merely a question of an outspoken journalist having strong opinions against the Russian system – as Mrs Fordeland does have – I cannot see that they would waste a moment over it, let alone have their principal intelligence functionary in London attending to the matter in person.'

'Are you completely sure that the lady has told you the truth, Sherlock – all of the truth?' asked Mycroft.

'One can never be absolutely certain that one has been told the truth, even when it is independently confirmed. I can only say that Mrs Fordeland strikes me as a lady who has a profound belief in honesty and plain-dealing. Would you not say so, Watson?'

'Oh indeed,' I agreed. 'I cannot imagine that the lady would willingly tell a lie, certainly not on her own behalf. I imagine, since she holds strong views on the treatment of the needy and powerless, that she might engage in dishonesty to protect another, but never herself.'

Holmes looked at me thoughtfully. 'I have said before, Watson, that you are not yourself luminous, but you transmit light. Whom do you imagine the lady might be defending?'

'I cannot imagine,' I said. 'It was merely a speculation that, if she has not revealed the truth to you, the reason will be the protection of somebody else, not herself.'

He nodded. 'You may be right,' he said, and I was pleased by his rare praise. 'Mrs Fordeland's secret, whatever it may be, must be connected with Russia and, *ergo*, with her time there or her articles about the country.'

'You sound very certain,' Mycroft commented.

'Tush, Mycroft. Surely the advancing years have not led you to a belief in coincidence? Was it not you, in our youth, who pointed out to me that, when two seemingly unconnected events occur in close proximity within the same frame of reference, a close and proper examination of the facts will reveal that they are connected? Here we have five people in London, two pairs of whom are manifesting a close but unexplained interest in the fifth. It must relate to the lady's time in Russia. What I fail to understand is the possible connection with the murder of Captain Parkes. That is why I should welcome a sight of your file, Mycroft.'

'And you are pursuing the Russian connection?' asked Mycroft.

'Of course!' exclaimed Holmes. 'At present I see no other direction to follow.'

Mycroft rose from his chair and gazed out of the window, with his back towards us. For several minutes he gazed down at the tree tops in the park below, all bright in their early summer greenery. At last he turned back to us, his mouth pursed.

'The Russians can be very difficult,' he remarked, seemingly apropos of nothing.

'I thought they were our allies,' I remarked.

'Ha!' he snorted. 'Allies! There are times when I would rather have every tribe of uncontrolled barbarians in the world as allies than Imperial Russia. Whatever they say, Doctor, they are almost always up to something else. They have never ceased to try and sneak into India and wrest it from us.'

He focused suddenly on his brother. 'Did you say that your client has an appointment with King Chula of Mongkuria? What is that about?'

'I imagine,' said Sherlock, 'that the meeting is purely social, merely a renewal of old acquaintance. After all, King Chula was her pupil as a child, and she seems to have been a great friend of her employer, King Chula's father.'

'You are sure of this?' demanded Mycroft.

'No, Mycroft, I am not. I merely believe that it is the most likely reason for their meeting. In my experience the most likely explanation is usually the correct one. Perhaps I am wrong and His Majesty wishes to make her the Mongkurian Ambassador to London.'

'We would not permit it!' snapped Mycroft, dropping back into his chair.

Holmes smiled. 'You take me too seriously, brother. I was jesting. The lady might make an admirable ambassador.'

'She is a damned meddler,' snorted Mycroft. 'She went to Mongkuria to teach the wives and children of the former King. He had a great many of both. In no time she was drafting correspondence with heads of state for him, attending his diplomatic meetings and advising him. It became an embarrassment. When he died and a regency took over during King Chula's minority, we were pleased to advise that her contract should not be renewed.'

'But why?' I exclaimed.

'I am sure, Doctor, that she acted out of her friendship with the King and a properly British sense of fair play, but it was an embarrassment to us.'

'You're not suggesting that she acted against British interests, are you?' I enquired.

'No,' he said. 'Not exactly. I grant you that she was instrumental in keeping the French and Germans out of Mongkuria. They wanted a way into Burma and India and Mongkuria seemed just the ideal backdoor. Her friend the King kept them at bay.'

'Then why do you complain?' asked Holmes.

'Because she treated all of us the same, that's why! While she was there, the King treated our fellows exactly the same as the French or Germans.'

Holmes nodded. 'And it became difficult for us to manufacture an excuse to take over his country and protect Burma and India. I see.'

There was a short silence, then Mycroft changed the direction of the conversation.

'It might be worth this department's while to find out what Kyriloff and Count Rimkoff are up to,' he said. 'Normally we leave Major Kyriloff alone. After all, he's usually interested in anarchists manufacturing bombs to throw at his masters. None of our affair, really, so long as they don't throw them here. When they do, it's a matter for Scotland Yard's Secret Branch. But Kyriloff and his unpleasant friend seem to be involved in something different. Perhaps I should know what it is. If it isn't our affair I can ignore it or pass it across to Scotland Yard. Yes, Sherlock. You may have a sight of our file on Captain Parkes. I shall have someone bring it round to your lodgings.'

Six

The Russian Interpreter

'I take it,' I said, as we sat in a hansom returning to Baker Street, 'that you will be able to make no further progress until you see Mycroft's file on the Parkes murder.'

'Whether I can make any further progress, Watson, remains to be seen,' he said, rather snappishly, I thought. 'What is clear is that it would be folly to do nothing until Mycroft's minions unearth a twenty-year-old file from their cumbersome archives.'

'Then what will you do?' I asked.

'In the absence of new data,' he said, 'there are two rational paths open to the enquirer. The first is to reconsider the existing data and see whether any new interpretation may be applied to it which will meet the facts. With your help and Mycroft's I have already reviewed Mrs Fordeland's problem and revealed a failure in my analysis of the data. You have pointed out to me that, while the lady does not present as a person who would lie or conceal information in her own interest, she might very well do so to protect someone else. I had failed to consider my own maxim that the absence of evidence does not prove that something has not occurred. I must now consider what Mrs Fordeland may be concealing and for what reason. I very much doubt that she will have misled us by inadvertence. The concealment, if there is one, will be deliberate and as a matter of principle.'

'And secondly?' I enquired.

'Secondly,' he said, 'the enquirer must consider whether there is a possibility of acquiring fresh data from an alternative source. It occurs to me that there is one avenue which I have not fully explored. That is the singular household of Miss Wortley-Swan.'

He looked at me thoughtfully. 'Tell me, Watson,' he said, 'you were quite certain that our client would not lie to us on her own account, and equally certain that she might do so to protect another. You will recall that I asked Mrs Fordeland if she knew of Miss Wortley-Swan. Do you think that she answered truthfully?'

I thought back to the look of perplexity which had crossed the lady's face when the name was mentioned to her. 'Yes,' I said. 'I am sure that she had never heard the name.'

He nodded. 'So am I, Watson, and that only adds to the singularity of the case.'

Mycroft's documents did not arrive during the remainder of the day, and I feared that Holmes might react with frustration to the delay, but I was wrong. It was a part of his remarkable structure of mind that, if unable to see a way ahead in an enquiry, he would rage with impatience and vent his feelings in a number of ways, including bizarre noises upon his violin which belied his love of music and his genuine skills and, in the past, recourse to cocaine.

On this occasion, however, having determined on a plan of action, he ate a hearty dinner and was an amiable companion throughout the evening, his conversation spreading as usual across a wide range of fascinating topics, every one of which he addressed as though he had made a special study of the subject.

There was no word from Mycroft on the following morning, but still Holmes seemed unruffled by the delay. It was not until after our luncheon that he pulled out his watch and remarked that we should be about our business if we were going to Sussex.

It was mid-afternoon when a stopping train from Victoria deposited us at the foot of the Sussex Downs, and a dog cart from the little station soon took us into Burriwell.

'You are not,' I said, as we drew up before a handsome villa set back from the road in spacious gardens, 'approaching her in disguise?'

'No,' he agreed. 'My elderly clergyman learned as much

as he might reasonably expect from the villagers. I have learned the effect of my profession and my reputation upon those who are concealing something, Watson. It seems to me that I should try it upon Miss Wortley-Swan.'

'You believe that the lady is concealing something?' I asked.

'I hope so, sincerely, Watson.'

The front doorbell was answered promptly by a plainly dressed maid, who showed us into a pleasant, sunny drawing room and took Holmes' card to her mistress. We were soon joined by the lady herself.

I do not believe that I ever had the pleasure of being introduced to her when she was the toast of England's young men, but I recall the engravings of her which appeared in the illustrated papers and the postcards of her which were sold in print shops. They showed her to be a tall woman of strong but delicate features with a head of golden hair. She wore a plain dress of light grey with very little jewellery. Now I saw that, though time had prematurely whitened her hair and she scorned to colour it artificially, she was still an upright and handsome figure.

When we had introduced ourselves she sent her maid for tea and waved us to chairs.

'No one,' she said, 'can be unaware of your profession and your reputation, Mr Holmes,' unconsciously echoing my friend's own words. 'Nevertheless, I find it impossible to see what enquiry has led you to my door.'

Holmes smiled. 'A great deal of the work which I do,' he said, 'consists in eliminating matters and people which have nothing to do with the focus of my enquiry. It may well be that this is such a matter. I am concerned in an enquiry on behalf of a lady visiting England for the Jubilee celebrations. In order to solve a matter which occasions her disquiet and maybe threatens her, it is necessary for me to identify a pair of people about whom I know nothing except that they are Russians and presently live within reasonable travelling distance of London.'

Miss Wortley-Swan laughed, a deep, musical sound. 'And you believe that my Gregori and his sister may be the ones you seek? I fear that you have wasted your journey, gentlemen.'

'Not if our visit serves to eliminate someone,' said Holmes, imperturbably. 'This Gregori is, then, a member of your household?'

The tea was served and we awaited an answer until it had been poured.

'Let me explain,' said our hostess. 'Since the brutal murder which robbed me of my intended husband, I have applied myself in efforts to improve the lot of those foreign refugees who, often through no fault of their own, find themselves taking refuge in this country. Many of them have no funds, sometimes no trade by which they may support themselves, and often they speak little or no English. I attempt to relieve those conditions and help them to become useful members of our society, helping themselves and our nation. It is difficult but rewarding work.'

She sipped her tea. 'You may imagine, Mr Holmes, that language is often a problem for me. I have learned a little Russian, but it is a very little and often not of the kind spoken by those I seek to aid. When I came across Gregori Gregorieff and his sister my problem was solved. Both of them are skilled linguists, not only in Russian but in other tongues, and to have their skills available to me has been a blessing. For that reason I have placed them on a small salary and removed them from a rather insalubrious lodging in Stepney to my own home, where they are readily available to me.'

She glanced at the mantelpiece clock. 'I expect that Gregori and his sister will be here at any moment. They were due to return by the train which, I suspect, brought you, but they will have walked from the railway station.'

She had barely spoken the words when we heard the sound of footsteps on the gravelled approach and the front door was opened and closed. There was a quiet murmur of voices in the hall, then the sound of someone ascending the stairs.

Miss Wortley-Swan stepped to the drawing-room door and called into the hall, 'Gregori, there are two gentlemen here who would be interested to meet you. Would you step in for a moment?'

She returned, followed by her Russian interpreter. Holmes' deductions had led me to expect the stocky and full-bearded man who appeared in Mrs Fordeland's sketch, perhaps unusually dressed. I was, therefore, taken completely by surprise.

The man who followed Miss Wortley-Swan into her drawing room was a short, not particularly stocky, man with only a small goatee beard. He wore pince-nez spectacles, secured by a black ribbon, and a cream linen jacket with grey flannels. In his left hand he held a narrow-brimmed straw hat.

'I am sorry,' he said to Miss Wortley-Swan, 'but Anna has developed a headache while upon the train. She has gone directly to her room. Did you wish to see both of us?'

'I shouldn't think that we need to bother her. Let me introduce my visitors, Gregori. They are Mr Sherlock Holmes, the well-known consulting detective, and his colleague, Dr Watson.'

I saw the quick flash of nervousness in the Russian's eyes before he composed his face in a smile and advanced to shake our hands. Once we were all seated, our hostess served tea to her interpreter and smiled around at us.

'I have been able,' she said, 'to convince Gregori of the virtues of the English cup of tea, as opposed to the strange brews that they serve in Russia, but I have never been able to woo him away from his devotion to strong Russian cigarettes. If you gentlemen would care to smoke, please feel free to do so.'

Immediately the Russian pulled out an ornate silver cigarette case and offered it. 'I am sorry,' he explained, 'that these are home-made. It is so difficult here in London to obtain a good Russian cigarette.'

Holmes rolled the cigarette between his long fingers, then sniffed at it. 'A strong Georgian and a Turkish blended,' he suggested, and the Russian smiled agreement.

'I see that you know your tobaccos, Mr Holmes. Tell me, into what are you enquiring at present?'

'I am seeking,' said Holmes, 'two persons, a man and a woman. I have descriptions of them and I am certain that they are Russian. So far I have been unsuccessful in my attempts to locate them. It was the knowledge that Miss Wortley-Swan had two Russian guests that prompted my enquiry, nothing more.'

The Russian glanced at his hostess, as though for approval. 'Miss Wortley-Swan will have told you that she employs me and my sister to help with her generous efforts among our fellow countrymen in London. Apart from assisting Miss Wortley-Swan, we have no other occupation. Both of us are anxious to make our home here in England now and we would certainly not do anything to cause concern to your excellent police force.'

I found his statement a little too glib, but Holmes appeared to have taken it at face value. He nodded and said, 'I am not, of course, a part of the official police. I am a consulting detective employed in the interests of a private citizen who has some concerns about the behaviour of this Russian pair. Tell me if you will, Mr Gegorieff, what caused you to leave Russia?'

The amiable expression on the Russian's face became solemn. 'You will be aware, Mr Holmes, that things in Russia are not as they are here. If a wrong is done, there may be no redress. A great wrong was done to my family and the perpetrator was a man of the nobility. My efforts to obtain justice angered him and life became extremely difficult for me and my sister. We thought it better to leave our country.'

Holmes nodded again. 'Since you have been in Britain,' he said, 'have you had any dealings with Major Kyriloff of the Russian Embassy?'

Gregorieff's expression turned to one of distaste and Miss Wortley-Swan emitted a most unladylike snort.

'That man!' she exclaimed. 'Major Kyriloff seems to imagine that every former citizen of Imperial Russia is a dedicated revolutionary, spending every day in schemes to murder the Tzar and overthrow the state! He and his agents are all over the poorer districts of London, harassing people whose only concern is to settle down in a strange country and make a living.'

'You have met him?' asked Holmes.

'Many times,' she declared, 'and he does not improve with acquaintance. His agents creep and spy among their unfortunate fellow countrymen in England, spreading lies and sowing money to create mischief. He is an unmitigated scoundrel!'

'You must,' said Holmes, 'hear a good deal of conversation about Kyriloff and his agents in the course of your work, Miss Wortley-Swan. Do you, by any chance, know what it is that most engages the major at present?'

'No,' she said, with a thoughtful expression. 'You are right that I hear a great deal of him, but at the moment he seems to have left the East End alone. Something else – and I do not know what – has taken up his time of late. I cannot say that the East End is sorry for his absence.'

My friend asked a few more, fairly perfunctory, questions of our hostess and her interpreter, then rose to take his leave. We were in the hall when he turned again to Miss Wortley-Swan.

'Forgive me,' he said, 'but you mentioned the brutal murder of your fiancé. I believe that his death remains unsolved?'

Her face tightened. 'Although it was twenty years ago,' she said, 'it is not a matter which I care to talk about. It is true that his death remains unsolved to this day. The wretched police of Paris chose to treat it as a random robbery by street bandits. Good afternoon, Mr Holmes, Doctor.'

It was a sunny afternoon and we made our way back to the little station on foot. Holmes was silent and I took it that he was disappointed by the afternoon's results.

'A wasted journey then, Holmes?' I ventured after a while.

'Nonsense!' he snapped. 'We have learned a great deal, or at least, I have.'

Seven

Conclusions and Obstacles

'So, Watson,' said Sherlock Holmes, as we sat back in our compartment on the train to Victoria, 'you believe that our visit to Miss Wortley-Swan was wasted?'

'Well, yes,' I said. 'Surely the purpose of your visit was to find the Russian who has been following Mrs Fordeland. Instead we found the lady's interpreter.'

My friend nodded and drew a paper from his coat pocket. 'And you believe that Mr Gregorieff is not our client's pursuer.' He held up the paper and placed a hand across its lower area. 'This,' he continued, 'is Mrs Fordeland's excellent sketch of her follower. Look at the eyes.'

'But,' I protested, 'the interpreter is slighter, bespectacled and wears only a goatee beard.'

'Look at the eyes,' he repeated. 'Imagine them behind pince-nez, ones which, incidentally, have only plain glass in them.'

I peered at the portrait as Holmes continued to mask the lower part of the face.

'You're right!' I exclaimed. 'The eyes are the same. Gregorieff could be a brother to the man in the drawing!'

Holmes snorted, and replaced the paper in his pocket. 'Watson,' he said, 'we are not talking about a brother here. Gregorieff is the same man.'

'But the build, the full beard!' I protested.

Holmes' exasperation with my slowness snapped. 'Great Heavens, Watson!' he exclaimed irritably. 'How many times over the years have you seen me adopt a disguise? And how many of those times have I made my features more rotund by pads inside my cheeks, or made my build more corpulent by padding beneath my clothing? No, Watson, Gregori Gregorieff, if that is really his name, is our man. If there were the least doubt in my mind, and there is not, there are two confirmatory circumstances.'

'What are they?' I asked, cautiously.

'Firstly, Mr Gregorieff's choice of tobacco. It is precisely the singular blend which our client's pursuer smokes, and it is rolled in identical cigarettes. Secondly, there is something which Mrs Fordeland herself told us. She said that, when she first became aware of the Russian couple, she thought that the man looked a little like an interpreter she had employed in Russia. It is hardly surprising that she failed to make the connection. Apart from Gregorieff's disguise, it is more than a quarter of a century since she was in Russia and she had, one imagines, no reason to suppose that Gregorieff was in London.'

'So Gregorieff was probably Mrs Fordeland's interpreter?' I asked.

'Excellent, Watson!' said my friend, sardonically. 'There is certainly something in Mrs Fordeland's past which involves Gregorieff. Something which she has chosen to conceal from us.'

'But she said that she did not recognize the bearded man and you appear to accept that she did not,' I protested.

'Certainly, Watson, I accept that she did not recognize him, but she glossed over her journey to Russia, making no importance of it. Yet it must be central to the entire mystery.'

He leaned forward earnestly and counted points off on his long fingers. 'Firstly,' he said, 'our client travelled in Russia years ago. Secondly, she is being followed by two Russians who turn out to be her former interpreter and, if we believe him, his sister. Thirdly, she is also followed by two agents of the Russian Embassy, one the devious and ruthless Major Kyriloff. Fourthly, Major Kyriloff went to the trouble of indicating to Mycroft that something with which I am dealing is of embarrassment to Russia.'

'We cannot be sure that he meant Mrs Fordeland's problem,' I said.

45

'Oh, we can, Watson, if only because I have no other enquiry in hand which has the remotest connection with Russia.' He paused. 'Nevertheless,' he continued, 'there is a fifth element present which I do not understand at all.'

'What is that?' I asked.

'The connection between Gregorieff and Miss Wortley-Swan. You saw it, Watson – the guarded glances between them and the carefully expressed answers. Their manner was that of co-conspirators guarding a secret, but I confess that I do not, at present, see what that secret may be.'

'It is evidently something with a Russian connection,' I observed.

'Very good, Watson,' he said – again sardonically.

I ignored my friend's attitude. 'Why do you imagine that the Russian Embassy is so interested in Mrs Fordeland?' I asked.

'We know why in part,' he replied. 'Skovinski-Rimkoff told Mycroft that my enquiry affects "the honour of his country". That country is in a very delicate state. It has a newly crowned Tzar, married to a German woman who is unpopular, both with the crowd and within the royal family. There are constant attempts at assassination of officials and even the Romanovs themselves. Many of those attempts are undoubtedly plotted in London and other foreign cities. It is little wonder that the odious Major Kyriloff is being pressed by a Romanov cousin. The catastrophe at Khodynka has raised animosity against the Tzar and his wife in a way nothing else could, Watson. It is a country drifting into serious danger and its rulers are frightened of their own shadows.'

'You are not suggesting that Mrs Fordeland has been plotting bomb outrages?' I asked.

'No, Watson, but Count Skovinsky-Rimkoff and Major Kyriloff evidently believe that she can embarrass their country in some way, and it has suffered enough embarrassment recently.'

I recalled the calamity at Khodynka Meadow, when a festival meant to celebrate Tzar Nicholas' coronation had turned into a tragedy as thousands were killed or injured in the crush. The Tzar's wife had been blamed for appearing at a French

Embassy ball on that night, and the people of Russia were already calling her 'the German bitch'.

'There is another matter which confuses me,' I said.

'Which is?' enquired Holmes.

'If you are right – and I'm sure you are – that Gregorieff is Mrs Fordeland's bearded man, she described him to us as often strangely dressed. I recall that she mentioned a striped blazer and a bowler hat. Yet Gregorieff appeared to us in perfectly ordinary garb, such as any respectable man might wear on a summer afternoon. Nor did he wear his false beard and his padding.'

'Aha!' exclaimed Holmes. 'So you were not asleep throughout the interview! Well done, Watson. Still, I have to point out that he might have changed his disguise on the train from London.'

'So he might,' I agreed, 'but there was no bag in the hall.'

'Very observant of you,' he said, 'but you have forgotten that his sister went upstairs immediately they arrived. She might well have removed a small bag containing the necessary items.'

'True,' I said, 'but on the occasion that you pursued him from Baker Street, you gave him no opportunity to change. Surely he did not arrive back in Burriwell in his peculiar costume?'

'But he did have an opportunity to change,' said Holmes. 'At Victoria I heard him take a ticket to Burriwell. We both boarded the local train, as today a non-corridor train. I certainly took the opportunity to adopt my clerical disguise in my compartment. I cannot say that he did not do the reverse, for I did not see him alight. I simply enquired about foreigners in the village, which led me to his address.'

I nodded, believing that my infant theory had been stifled. 'Then you think that he sets out in ordinary clothing, but changes on the train?' I asked.

Holmes shook his head. 'I did not say so. It would be impractical. In the first place he could not guarantee always having a compartment by himself, unless he reserved one, which would draw attention to him. In the second place, to repeatedly appear at the station in ordinary garb and in London in a more peculiar form, might eventually draw the attention of someone who would wonder what he is about.'

He took his cigarette case from his pocket and offered it across. 'I entirely agree with you, Watson, that the man has a bolthole somewhere in London. If he did not flee there when I followed him, it was because he did not wish to run the risk of me knowing where it is. He was safe in fleeing to Burriwell, because he knew that Miss Wortley-Swan would support him in the face of any enquiry I made – as she has done.'

'Then you propose to seek his London *pied-a-terre*?' I said, delighted that for once I had come to the right conclusion.

'Certainly,' he said, 'but before that there are other measures to be taken, and, like you, there is still a matter which perplexes me.'

'What matter is that?' I asked.

'While we are agreed that there is some unrevealed purpose in the connection between Gregorieff and his employer, I have not the least indication of where that purpose lies, Watson.'

He emphasized his remark by rapping his stick on the carriage floor, then stared thoughtfully out of the window, remaining silent until we reached Victoria. At the cab rank I was surprised when Holmes turned aside, leaving me to travel home to Baker Street alone.

'You go on, Watson,' he said. 'There are arrangements which I must make.'

It was some time before he rejoined me at our lodgings, but his manner had that lightness which I had learnt to interpret as a sign of progress in his enquiry. We passed a pleasant dinner and he would, no doubt, have continued in the same mood, but for the arrival of a messenger from Mycroft's department.

The courier had brought the official file on the murder of Captain Parkes, and initially Holmes fell upon it eagerly. However, as he leafed through its many pages, he began to emit snorts of impatience and muttered comments.

'Useless!' he exclaimed, flinging the folder to the floor and reaching for his pipe. 'They are worse than Scotland Yard. They have overlooked absolutely everything that might have been of importance.'

'The French police?' I asked.

'Indeed,' said Holmes. 'But our own investigators were as bad.'

'Were they not Scotland Yarders?' I enquired.

'No!' he said. 'They might have been bad enough, but Mycroft's underlings did not wish to embarrass the Paris police, so they sent only a retired officer to discuss the case with the French. He confined himself to reading the statements taken by the French and listening to their opinions, and came back to recommend that their conclusions be accepted – that it was a random killing by street bandits.'

'Are there indications that it was not?' I asked.

'Consider, Watson. Captain Parkes was a fit young man and, having been to a diplomatic ball, was dressed in the more than ordinately decorative formal uniform of his rank and regiment. Why on earth would a street bandit risk an encounter with a man whose uniform proclaimed him as skilled in fighting?'

'No,' I agreed. 'I imagine that they would avoid such a man.'

'Precisely, Watson! Street garrotters in any city are cowardly vermin who prey upon the weak and unwary.'

'Was he, perhaps, drunk?' I hazarded.

'It is in the highest degree unlikely,' said Holmes. 'He had attended an important diplomatic ball as escort to his newly acquired fiancée and had been in the presence of his superiors.'

'Nevertheless, he may have been,' I persisted. 'I was a young officer myself once. I am not forgetful of their capabilities for foolish conduct.'

'Ah!' he said. 'I always forget your illustrious military career, Watson. Can you recall, from your experience, a captain becoming seriously inebriated in the presence of his fiancée and his superiors at an important function?'

'Well, no,' I said, after a moment's thought. 'There was the occasion when Lieutenant Harrington misbehaved himself at Aldershot.'

'A lieutenant,' interjected Holmes. 'Was he with his fiancée or any other lady?'

'Well, no, but . . .'

'Was he observed by his superiors?' demanded Holmes.

'Well, no, but . . .'

He flung up an imperious hand. 'Enough!' he said. 'You make my point.'

He drummed his fingers impatiently on the arm of his chair. 'Not only,' he said, 'does Mycroft's file contain nothing that will assist in my investigation, there is one piece of information which indicates a considerable obstacle.'

'What is that?' I enquired.

'There was a Captain Wilmshaw in Paris at the time, a friend of the murdered man. He was the man who identified the body. There is a statement from Wilmshaw in the file. It is completely useless. It merely sets out that he was an old friend of the dead man, that he was present at the ball and saw Parkes there with his fiancée, and recalls the time at which Parkes and Miss Wortley-Swan left. He says that he shared digs in Paris with Parkes and that he became concerned when Parkes failed to come home that night. After the ball he never saw his friend again until he was taken to the mortuary to identify his remains.'

'You would have wished to question this man, I imagine, about Parkes' mood, his associates, events at the ball and so on.'

'Very good, Watson. That is exactly so.'

'But is he not now available? Is he dead?'

'He might as well be,' said Holmes bitterly. 'Mycroft has appended a note to the file to say that Wilmshaw is now a colonel and has been serving in the Sudan, where he remains.'

He drummed his fingers once more, then broke out again. 'If I had been consulted at the time, Watson, there are two people that I would have wished to question very closely – Captain Wilmshaw and Miss Wortley-Swan. The French police – no doubt in a demonstration of French romantic delicacy – did not even question Miss Wortley-Swan! The fools!'

'Surely that is understandable,' I suggested.

'Understandable?' he snarled. 'It is nothing less than crass incompetence! They allowed the lady to tell them – through the British Embassy – the time and address at which she and

Captain Parkes parted and that he intended to walk home because it was a fine night. She had been with him all evening, she was the last person known to have seen him alive and the idiots did not question her!'

He prodded the scattered file with a contemptuous foot. 'Worthless!' he snorted. 'Worthless!'

I recalled Agatha Wortley-Swan as I had first seen her, in her photographs and engravings of twenty years before. 'She was a very beautiful young woman,' I said, 'who had just suffered a calamitous loss. I imagine that they did not wish to press her.'

'Press her?' he repeated. 'They never even spoke to her, Watson. How often have you and I had to deal with those in grief and press them for facts which will help us to reveal the truth? In the immediate aftermath of murder it is necessary to treat every witness as a potential killer, not least those whose relationship with the victim was a close one.'

'You are not suggesting,' I said, genuinely shocked, 'that the French police should have treated Miss Wortley-Swan as a suspect, surely?'

'Why not?' he said. 'Why not? On the material assembled in their inadequate enquiry it would be possible to base a theory that the lady had taken some extreme exception to marrying Captain Parkes but did not wish to be seen to break off their engagement. *Ergo*, she paid a gang of street assassins to murder him.'

'But you cannot possibly believe that, Holmes!'

'Of course not, Watson. I was merely demonstrating what I have remarked to you before – that, where the data is inadequate, almost any theory may be erected without contradiction. If only my confounded brother had called me in at the time!'

'I seem to recall that your brother referred to Captain Parkes' death as a "minor incident",' I said. 'Maybe he did not see any point in troubling you. Besides, it was twenty years ago. Were you in practice then?'

'I had been in practice as a consulting detective for some two years when this "minor incident" occurred, Watson. Mycroft had already consulted me more than once.'

There was a half-formed but disturbing thought in my head. I decided that it was better to bring it into the open. 'I wonder,' I said, 'if our government did not press the French over this matter because they did not wish to know the answer.'

My friend looked at me with a thoughtful expression for a long moment. Then he said, 'I underestimate you sometimes, Watson. You may be entirely right.'

Eight

A Shot in the Park

The following morning was a Sunday, and I made it the excuse to rise late, at least in part because I foresaw that Holmes' mood was unlikely to have improved since the previous evening. Late as I was, however, Sherlock Holmes was later. I was well into my breakfast when he entered, still in his dressing gown and holding Mycroft's file under one arm.

He dropped the file on his desk, gave me a curt greeting, sat down at the table and poured himself a cup of coffee. For several minutes he sipped his coffee without remark, making no attempt to serve himself from the covered dishes on the table. Silently I offered him the toast, but he waved it away. I noted his lack of appetite as an almost invariable indication that he thought his deductive process to have faltered or stopped.

After a while he emitted a long sigh. 'Watson,' he said, 'I almost convinced myself last night that the French police could not have been as slipshod as they were. I took Mycroft's papers to my bed and wasted much time in reconsidering them, but I was right in the first place. The veriest tyro at Scotland Yard could not have done worse.'

'I do not recall,' I said, trying to divert him into specifics rather than a general complaint, 'how Captain Parkes died.'

'There you have it, Watson. The answer is that we do not know. The file says merely that "it is believed" that Parkes was killed by a blow to the head from behind, inasmuch as there was a crushing injury to his skull. On the other hand there were other injuries, slashing and stabbing wounds, some

53

of which may have been inflicted by two or more different knives, but he had been several days in the river and any or all of those injuries may have occurred in the water.'

'It should,' I said, 'have been possible, unless the body had actually begun to decay, to make a reasonable judgement as to which injuries were deliberate and which were inflicted by obstacles in the river post mortem.'

'Precisely so, Watson, precisely so, but your French colleague made no such attempt. All we have is a rough sketch of the location of the injuries, which might indicate that Parkes was attacked by two or three men armed with knives and eventually struck down from behind. We do not know if he died from stabbing or from the blow to the head. Dr Legrange tends to the latter view. He is, at least, certain that the captain did not drown.'

I was trying to find some positive aspect of the matter to raise his spirits, but it was not easy. 'You said,' I recalled, 'that the two persons that you would most have wished to question were Miss Wortley-Swan and Captain Parkes' friend Wilmshaw. Colonel Wilmshaw may not be available, but surely you could talk to Miss Wortley-Swan?'

'So I could, Watson, so I could, and she would undoubtedly lie to me again, as she did yesterday, if only by omission. Besides, while she was quite willing to mention her murdered fiancé to a total stranger at the beginning of our interview, you will have noted that, as we were leaving, it became a subject that she found too distressing to discuss.'

He sipped at his coffee, found the cup empty and poured himself a fresh cup which he drank in two gulps. Rising from the table, he flung himself on to the couch and reached for his pipe.

Once I was certain that he had settled into a long silence, I took a chair by the window and began to read.

It was a fine, warm day and the usual commercial clatter of traffic in Baker Street had been stilled by the Sabbath. With the shops and offices closed, the only sounds were of pedestrians, many of them families making their way up to the park for a pleasant afternoon. Through the open window came the sound of their footfalls and snatches of conversation, bursts of children's laughter and only occasionally the sound of wheels.

The late-morning sun shone full into the windows of our sitting room and I enjoyed its warmth. Much as I enjoyed accompanying my friend on his enquiries, I was quite prepared to enjoy a sunny day with a good book, for it was comparatively rarely that we were disturbed on a Sunday.

I had read for some time when Holmes uncoiled himself from the couch, knocked out his pipe on the fender and came to stand silently beside me at the window. As he said nothing, I continued with my reading.

'Hullo!' he exclaimed, suddenly. 'What's this?' He peered towards the Marylebone Road and I stretched in my seat to look. I had heard the rumble of a four-wheeler cab, driven at speed, and soon I heard it jerk to a halt beneath our window.

'That's Lestrade,' announced Holmes, and I saw that his face had lightened at the prospect of a fresh problem. 'Perhaps I had better dress,' he announced and made for his bedroom.

Moments later Mrs Hudson was at our door, accompanied by the scent of roasting lamb from her kitchen to remind me that it would soon be time for luncheon. A sweating Inspector Lestrade also followed her, his usually sallow face red and a kerchief in his hand.

'Doctor,' he greeted me. 'I hope that I have found Mr Holmes in. There's been a shooting in Hyde Park.'

Sherlock Holmes, dressed as carefully as though he had a valet's assistance, stepped through the internal door. 'Take the basket chair, Lestrade,' he invited, and stepped to the gasogene to pour the little inspector a generous brandy.

Lestrade almost fell into the chair and grasped gratefully at the drink, taking it down in two swallows.

'There's been a shooting in Hyde Park,' he repeated when he had drunk. 'It's a Russian nob, here for the Jubilee.'

Holmes flung me a quick glance under his eyebrows, and I noticed that his right hand began to stroke the ball of his left thumb, as he did when he expected excitement.

'Calm down, Lestrade,' he commanded. 'There has been a shooting of a Russian in Hyde Park. So much we have gathered.

Now – who is the Russian, is he dead and who has shot at him?'

The inspector felt in his pockets and produced his notebook, thumbing through it quickly. Eventually he said, 'It is a Count Stepan Skovinski-Rimkoff,' mangling the pronunciation horribly.

Holmes flung me another quick glance, which I interpreted as a warning to say nothing that might reveal our interest in the victim.

'He is a nob, you say?' pressed Holmes. 'A visitor to the Jubilee?'

'Worse,' said Lestrade. 'He's not only a visitor to the ceremony – according to Major Kyriloff, he's a cousin of the new Tzar.'

'Ah!' exclaimed Sherlock Holmes. 'So, Major Kyriloff is already involved. I do not understand, Lestrade, why your commisioner allows that man to stay at liberty. He is responsible for a significant percentage of the violent crime in this city, yet Scotland Yard lets him run free.'

'You know perfectly well why it is, Mr Holmes,' said Lestrade, looking hurt. 'We should be very happy to feel the major's collar, but your brother's department won't let us.'

'And that,' said Holmes, 'is simply because Kyriloff would be replaced immediately by some other agent of the Tzar, and my brother's minions would be put to the trouble of finding out who it was.'

'I can't sit and argue politics with you, Mr Holmes. I've got a very indignant Russian toff in Hyde Park, making a noise, not to mention the aforesaid Kyriloff hanging about being insulting. I would welcome your views on the matter, if you can spare the time,' said Lestrade.

Holmes lifted both hands in apology. 'Forgive me, Lestrade. Of course, Watson and I will be delighted to accompany you. You may fill us in on the way.'

Mrs Hudson intercepted us at the stair's foot. 'I see you are on your way, Mr Holmes,' she said. 'I was about to serve luncheon. May I take it that it will not now be needed?'

'I'm so sorry, Mrs Hudson,' said Holmes, 'but the inspector

has an emergency which affects Her Majesty's Jubilee. We must go at once.'

Lestrade's cab was still at the kerb and we piled aboard. 'Now,' commanded Sherlock Holmes, once we were seated and the vehicle pulled away, 'be so kind as to outline the facts, Lestrade.'

Lestrade reached for his pocketbook again. 'It appears,' he said, 'that this Russian gentleman and Major Kyriloff were riding in Rotten Row. They had gone slowly up the Row, east to west, as it were, and had turned and come back. About two thirds of their way back, a shot was fired at the count.'

'Was he hit?' asked Holmes.

Lestrade shook his head. 'No,' he said. 'The shot startled his horse, making it rear, and the count fell heavily. I think he's dislocated his shoulder where he fell.'

'One shot only?' asked Holmes.

'That's it,' said the inspector.

'What became of the person who fired it?'

'He got away,' said Lestrade. 'He'd been behind some shrubbery. What with the shot, it startled the crowd and the horses, so there was a fair old confusion at first. There were people running away and people coming to see and ladies and gentlemen trying to calm their horses down. He must have got away in all that.'

'This one shot,' said Holmes, 'how do we know that it was fired at Count Skovinski-Rimkoff, since it didn't hit him?'

The little policeman gazed at Holmes for a moment without answering. Then he said, 'Well, that's what the count and Major Kyriloff say.'

'And where were they in relation to the shooter?'

'We have a small boy who saw the smoke and heard the shot in the shrubbery. From what he says, the man with the gun was about fifty yards ahead of the Russians, on their left front.'

'So he might have fired at either with very little difference to his chances,' observed Holmes.

'I suppose that's true, Mr Holmes, but both the Russians seem convinced that the count was the target.'

'Has it not occurred to you, Lestrade, that Major Kyriloff

is certainly the most hated Russian in London – at least by his fellow countrymen? Faced with a clear shot at Kyriloff or the count, I would have expected the choice to be Kyriloff.'

'Then, what do you make of the fact that it wasn't?' asked Lestrade.

'We do not know that it wasn't, Lestrade. The reliability of evidence must be measured against its source, and I would not regard Major Kyriloff as a reliable source. The count I do not know. Do you know any more about the matter?'

'No, Mr Holmes,' said Lestrade. 'Once Major Kyriloff had told me who the count was and that he was invited for the Jubilee, I thought that I would welcome your views on the affair.'

In other words, I thought to myself, finding himself out of his depth, the little inspector had run to Baker Street for my friend's assistance, as he so often did.

It may be that Sherlock Holmes was thinking along similar lines. 'Tell me,' he asked Lestrade, 'how you come to be mixed up in this. Surely an assassin's shot at a visitor to the Jubilee is more a matter for the Secret Department at the Yard?'

'So it would be ordinarily,' agreed the detective, 'but with London crawling with all manner of royalty and politicians from all over the world, the Secret Department can't cope. A whole lot of us have been told off to assist them. I was assigned particularly, because of my success ten years ago against that madman's plot at the Golden Jubilee, which I freely admit was down to you, Mr Holmes.'*

We had no opportunity to discuss the matter further, for we were arriving at the park.

* See *Sherlock Holmes and the Royal Flush*, Constable & Co.

Nine

Smoke Without Fire

Largest of the capital's parks, Hyde Park is of great importance as a place of recreation to multitudes in our crowded city. Originally created in the days of Henry VIII, the narrow-spirited Parliament under dictator Cromwell sold it to private owners. Everyone who so much as walks his dog there or simply sits upon the grass in the sun, should thank Charles II that he recovered the park when the monarchy was restored.

On a fine day there is no more populous or popular part of the park than the ride known as 'Rotten Row' or the 'Ladies' Mile'. This tree-lined ride, along the south side of the park, was (and still remains) the favourite resort of fashionable Londoners who wish to take a little gentle equestrian exercise and, at the same time, to see and by seen by their fellows.

For hours at a time, the Row becomes a slow-moving procession of smart young men, dressed to the nines, and, more particularly, of the most beautiful and best-dressed women in the world. Groups and individuals exchange greetings and pleasantries as they pass and repass, and quite frequently assignations are made by a gesture, the movement of a gloved hand on the bridle or a significant handling of the whip. Indeed, while the mounted parade includes many members of society and well-known performers, there is no doubt that more than a few of the exquisite lovelies who ornament the scene are ladies of the demi-monde.

It can be imagined that this parade of fashion and style is treated as a free exhibition by Londoners who, if they cannot afford to participate, loiter along the edges of the Row to admire and comment upon the passing show.

The sunny day had brought a large crowd, of riders and onlookers, and it was at the heart of this that the incident involving Count Skovinski-Rimkoff had occurred, so that it took us no little while to force a way through the throng and reach the area, cordoned by Lestrade's constables, where the count and Major Kyriloff awaited us.

The Russian nobleman sat with his back to the bole of a tree, smoking a cigarette, his arm in a makeshift sling created from a large silk handkerchief, while Kyriloff paced up and down in front of him. The major looked up as we approached and said something to the count.

Skovinski-Rimkoff struggled awkwardly to his feet as we approached. 'At last!' he exclaimed, 'Scotland Yard has produced its fabled investigator. How do you do, Mr Holmes. I have met your brother recently.'

'So I understand,' said Holmes, 'but I should make it completely clear that I am not a member of the official police. I am a consulting detective in private practice. I am here entirely at Inspector Lestrade's suggestion.'

'Of course,' replied the Russian, sardonically. 'A private consulting detective, yet you carry out enquiries for your powerful brother. Were you not involved in the affair of the South African telegram last year?'

'If I had been,' said Holmes, 'I would not be in a position to discuss it.'

Major Kyriloff intervened. 'Inspector Lestrade, this delay is intolerable. Count Stepan has received only the crudest medical aid since the incident, and you keep us here in this park where there may be other assassins for all that we know.'

He looked around him nervously, as though every bush held a killer. 'Perhaps,' suggested Holmes, 'Dr Watson may examine the count while Major Kyriloff explains to me what has happened here.'

'What has happened here is an attempt to murder a cousin of His Imperial Highness Tzar Nicholas, and your police are treating it as of no consequence!' declared Kyriloff.

'Major Kyriloff,' said Holmes, with that very even tone which I knew to conceal considerable anger, 'it is immaterial to me whether you wish this matter dealt with or whether you prefer to retreat to your Embassy and write letters of protest to the Foreign Office. I have asked you for the facts, not your opinions.'

'Count Stepan and I were taking a leisurely ride here when some murderous madman fired at him,' said the Russian.

'Do you or the count ride often in the Row?' asked Holmes.

'Not often, no,' said Kyriloff.

'And today?' pressed Holmes.

'The count had said that he remembered riding in the Row when he was in London years ago. He wished to do so again and I agreed to accompany him.'

'Ah, yes,' responded my friend. 'I had not forgotten that Count Skovinski-Rimkoff has been in London before and sampled the city's social life. So, you had agreed to ride today. Who would have known of that intention?'

'My own staff, others at the Embassy, the count's personal staff, the stable which provided the horses, many people.'

'You had, I believe, been up the Row and were returning,' said Holmes. 'Did anything at all untoward occur as you went up the ride? You were not shot at then?'

'Of course not!' snapped the Russian. 'There was no disturbance at all as we went in that direction.'

'It serves to establish that your attacker was most probably not in position when you went up the Row,' said Holmes. 'You had returned to this point when the incident occurred. Tell me what happened – precisely.'

'We were moving along the ride, a few feet behind the party in front of us, which was two young men and two ladies. I admit that I was not looking about. I was lighting a cigarette when I heard the shot. It came from over there,' and he pointed to a clump of shrubbery.

'I was, of course, immediately concerned for the safety of Count Stepan. He had been riding on my left. I saw that his horse had reared and that he had thrown himself from the saddle to avoid the shot . . .'

Holmes interrupted him. 'He had thrown himself from the saddle,' he repeated. 'He was not, then, unseated by his horse rearing?'

'Of course not!' said the major. 'The count is a superb

horseman. His horse reared at the shot, but Count Stepan had already flung himself to the ground.'

Holmes nodded. 'And what did you do, Major?'

'I sprang from the saddle and looked to see if the count was injured. When I saw that he had not been shot but had injured his shoulder, I helped him to the side of the ride and spoke to a police officer who had arrived.'

'And there was only one shot?' said Holmes.

'I have said so,' replied the Russian.

'Why do you think that was?' asked Holmes.

The Russian looked at him with a puzzled expression. 'How would I know?' he said. 'I cannot fathom the behaviour of madmen.'

'Really?' said Sherlock Holmes. 'I had thought that you were in the business of trying to fathom the minds of madmen, but it makes no matter. Why do you imagine that Count Stepan was the target?'

'A ridiculous question!' snorted the major. 'Of course he was the target! A member of our Imperial family in front of some lunatic with a gun – who else would be the target?'

'It occurs to me, Major, that amongst your fellow countrymen in England you must be easily the most hated and feared. Why would you imagine that you were not the intended victim?'

'I do not understand you, Mr Holmes. I do my duty for my country here in London, which is to protect her from the machinations of the rabble of Jews, Socialists and Anarchists who take refuge here and who your government and your police allow to flourish like weeds.'

'Of course,' said Holmes. 'Watson, how is the count?'

'Very well, considering,' I said. 'I feared that he had dislocated his shoulder when he hit the ground, but he had merely displaced some muscle tissue which became trapped by his shoulder blade. A little pressure has replaced it. He will be as right as rain tomorrow when the bruised muscle eases.'

Holmes nodded and turned to Lestrade. 'I hope,' he said. 'that your fellows have prevented anyone from trampling over the ground – and have not done so themselves.'

'As soon as I got here I gave orders that nothing was to be disturbed, Mr Holmes. I was intending to invite you along and I know how particular you are about things being left as they were.'

'Very good,' said my friend, 'Now, where is your witness – the small boy?'

Lestrade led us to a ragged lad of about nine years, who was squatting at the feet of a watchful sergeant. As we approached, the boy stood up.

'The sergeant says as there might be a reward in it,' he announced hopefully to Holmes.

'So there may,' said Holmes, fingering the coins in his pocket, 'but only if you tell us the exact truth about what you have seen. Now, did you see the shot fired?'

'Not exactly,' said our informant, 'but I heard it and I saw the smoke and I saw a bloke running away behind the shrubbery afterwards.'

'Excellent!' exclaimed Holmes. 'Now, will you be kind enough to show me where all this happened?'

He put a hand on the urchin's shoulder and let the boy lead him into the shrubbery that bordered the ride. From time to time I caught glimpses of him poking about with his stick behind the bushes and once I saw him showing his guide a piece of paper. Quite soon they emerged, the boy grinning broadly and testing a half-sovereign with his teeth, and Holmes with an expression of satisfaction.

'You may let the lad go,' he told Lestrade. 'He has been most informative.' He gazed about him. 'I imagine,' he said, 'that you have not found any bullet that was fired?'

'No, Mr Holmes,' replied the inspector, 'but, of course, the assassin would have been crouched in those bushes and firing upwards at the count on his horse. The bullet, having missed its mark, would have travelled on upwards. It might have landed anywhere in the park once it was spent.'

'Oh, indeed,' agreed Holmes. 'I was not suggesting that you look for it. There are, however, some footprints in the shrubbery which you may find interesting. It is, perhaps, worth having a cast made of them, although I have a good description of the man who made them.'

'You have a description of the perpetrator from the boy?' asked Lestrade.

'Better,' said Holmes, but I think I am done here now. Would you have one of your men call a cab? Perhaps, if it is not inconvenient, you might like to take pot luck with us at Baker Street?'

A gabble of excited Russian broke out between the count and Major Kyriloff, then Kyriloff strode over, his face angry.

'Do I understand that you are leaving, Mr Holmes?'

'You do, Major,' said Holmes. 'I have, I believe, collected all the data that is of any use here and drawn certain conclusions.'

'Then you must let us know what are your conclusions,' demanded the Russian.

'I must do no such thing,' said Holmes, evenly. 'I was called into consultation in this matter by Inspector Lestrade. I will, in due course, make my views known to him. In the meantime there is nothing I can usefully do here.'

'But you have not even asked for a description of the man who fired the shot!' exclaimed Kyriloff.

'I do not think that I need to enquire,' said Holmes. 'I rarely guess, but let me do so now. After the shot was fired and the count plunged to the ground, you sprang down and saw to the count, but this did not prevent you seeing someone run away from behind that shrubbery. Am I correct?'

'That is exactly the case,' agreed Kyriloff, in a very strange tone of voice.

Holmes nodded. 'And the man that you saw was of medium height, stocky and with a full dark beard. In addition, he was eccentrically dressed, perhaps in a striped blazer and bowler hat. Am I correct? Was that the man, Major?'

Kyriloff's eyes had widened at my friend's recital, but now they narrowed suspiciously. 'How do you know that?' he snapped.

'It is a part of my business to know things, Major Kyriloff, and, like yours, it is also a part not to reveal how I know them. Good afternoon. Come, Watson, Inspector.'

He tipped his hat to Kyriloff and the count, who fell to arguing furiously again in Russian as we strolled away.

Ten

Sherlock Holmes Explains

When I had first joined forces with Holmes, some eighteen years before, to take up the occupancy of our diggings in Baker Street, I admit that I was mostly concerned to find accommodation that would not strain my slender financial resources. I had no knowledge of my companion's unique profession, his astonishing mental abilities, nor of his personal habits. It was some time before I grasped these facts and longer yet before I realized how extremely fortunate Holmes had been in finding a suite of rooms that so exactly met his requirements and were overseen by a landlady like Mrs Hudson, for surely no other woman in London, if not in the whole of England, would have suffered Holmes' idiosyncrasies as calmly as our long-suffering hostess.

When we arrived back at Baker Street, with Lestrade in tow, she met us in the hall and simply enquired if it was now convenient to serve our meal and was the inspector to join us. Within minutes our table was laid and all three of us were enjoying the cold fruits of that roast I had smelled earlier, with suitable accompaniments. Holmes opened a bottle of a pleasant wine and chatted wittily throughout our meal, though without once mentioning the day's events in Hyde Park.

I was pleased to see Holmes' lightened mood and glad that Lestrade's summons had served to distract my friend from his frustration, but I was mystified also by the incident in the park and as anxious as Lestrade to know what conclusions Holmes had drawn.

The continental habit of taking coffee after dinner had not then taken root in England, so that it was with another glass that we each retreated from the table when our meal was done. Holmes lit a favourite cherry, I took a cigarette and the inspector accepted the offer of a cheroot from the selection which Holmes kept in the coal scuttle. When we had all lit up, Lestrade and I looked expectantly at Holmes.

'Well now, Watson,' he began, 'what do you make of today's little adventure?'

'It makes no sense,' I said. 'While I do not pretend to have seen as far into the affair as you, Holmes, I can see that the account given by Kyriloff and the count does not make sense.'

He nodded silently and I went on. 'Even if they are right – if the attack was intended against the count, not Kyriloff, the gunman had both of them within yards only. Surely he would have tried for both?'

Holmes nodded again. 'Indeed,' he said, 'yet only one shot was heard. Skovinski-Rimkoff, we know, has not been in Britain for years, and though he left a disgruntled victim here, that was a woman. It would be much more likely that Major Kyriloff, well known and well hated among the Russian émigré community in London, was the target, but both he and the count assert that the count was the intended victim, and neither of them can explain their certainty.'

It was our turn to nod, though I noticed Lestrade's surprise at Holmes' knowledge of the Russian count's unsavoury past.

'Let us,' said Holmes, 'leave the question of which was the target and consider the single shot. Major Kyriloff, who admits he was lighting a cigarette at the time, says that the count flung himself from the saddle to avoid the shot. I confess that I wonder what, precisely, the major means by that.'

'Well,' said Lestrade, 'I assumed that he meant that the count heard the shot and leapt from his horse.'

'That,' said Holmes, 'might avoid a second shot, but could not possibly avoid the first shot.'

Lestrade looked puzzled.

'Come now, Lestrade, all of us here have had the pleasure of being fired on. Watson can remind you that old soldiers say that you may see the flash of the bullet that kills you, but you will never hear the explosion. Count Stepan, we are asked to believe, is an exception to that rule of nature. If he leapt from his horse when he heard the shot, he would have been too late. The bullet would, in all probability, have hit him before he jumped. Even if he saw the flash of the shot and jumped, he would have been too late.'

'But,' I said, for I did not fully understand Holmes' point, 'what if the assassin missed his shot? Suppose the count acted by reflex, not by thought, and the shot would have missed him in any case?'

Holmes drew on his pipe. 'A possibility, Watson, I grant you, but an extremely slender one. You have seen how close the horses were to the assassin. He had a clear target, moving slowly towards him at a very short distance. There is no reason why he should have missed. On the other hand, there are two reasons why neither the count nor Major Kyriloff was hit.'

Lestrade was as puzzled as I was. 'I don't quite follow all this, Mr Holmes. Why would they not have been hit?'

Holmes smiled. 'If there was no shot,' he said.

'No shot!' both the inspector and I exclaimed at once. 'But the boy, and others, heard the shot!' I continued.

'Not so, Watson, not so. I was most cautious in my questioning of the lad and he was most careful in repeating what he saw. He said that he had been loitering against a tree near the shrubbery, watching the riders and looking for a chance to earn a coin by holding a horse or carrying a message. He became aware of a man slipping into the bushes, but thought no more than that he had stepped in there to answer a call of nature. However, rustling noises made him aware that the man was moving among the bushes and young Freddy, for that is the youth's name, caught a glimpse of someone stooping down in the heart of the shrubs. His attention was still drawn to the riders in the main, as was that of everyone else.'

He paused and drew on his pipe. 'That,' he said, 'is worth remembering.'

'You mean that the lad was not paying much attention?' enquired Lestrade.

'No,' said Holmes. 'I mean that the bystanders were there to watch the riders and the riders were there to watch each other. As a result, no one except young Freddy was paying any attention at all to the man in the bushes.'

'That's understandable,' I remarked. 'If you go out to watch the riders in Rotten Row you hardly expect some lunatic to be lurking behind the shrubs with murder on his mind.'

'Certainly not,' agreed Holmes, 'but consider what occurred next. According to Freddy, and I can see no reason to doubt him, he stayed close to the shrubbery and was still there when he smelt smoke. He was wondering where it came from when he heard the sound of a gun nearby.'

'He must be wrong!' exclaimed Lestrade. 'That cannot be right.'

'Why not, pray?' asked my friend.

'Well, he's not remembered it properly,' said the inspector. 'He says that there was a smell of smoke and then there was a gunshot. Numbers of other persons have told my officers that they heard the shot and then they saw smoke drifting from the shrubbery. He's got it wrong.'

'I would agree with you, Lestrade, that it is of the utmost importance to keep events in the correct sequence, but can you tell me if any other witness was as near the shrubbery as Freddy, or noticed a man there before the gunshot?'

'Well, no,' said the little policeman. 'The boy was the nearest one to the shrubbery that we could find, but he must be wrong.'

'It is also,' said Holmes, 'of the utmost importance to avoid disbelieving a witness simply because their evidence does not fit a preconceived theory of the incident.'

I began to have some slight idea of where Holmes was taking us.

'You said earlier,' I recalled, 'that the story told by Kyriloff and the count would only make sense if there was no shot. Is that what you believe, Holmes?'

'Excellent, Watson!' exclaimed Sherlock Holmes. 'That is not only what I believe, it is what I know.'

Lestrade was gaping in amazement. 'But umpteen people heard the shot,' he said.

Holmes shook his head. 'No, Lestrade. A large number of people, every one of whom was concerned with something else and not expecting a shot from the shrubbery, heard what sounded like a pistol shot. They looked and saw smoke drifting from the shrubbery. Meanwhile, Count Stepan had made his dramatic plunge out of the saddle and Kyriloff had leapt to assist him. The onlookers heard a sound, saw smoke drifting and a man fell from his horse. What more natural than that they should believe a shot had been fired – as indeed they were supposed to do.'

He knocked out his pipe on the grate. 'I have told both of you, on numerous occasions, that the most likely explanation is usually the correct one. This is an interesting example of that argument being turned on its head. Someone who understands the processes of investigation has played on that factor to produce a false impression, to create a body of completely honest witnesses who will assert that a shot was fired.'

'Who would have done that?' I asked. 'Kyriloff? But he was in full view, on horseback alongside the count.'

'It has a certain smack of the major about it,' agreed Holmes. 'He probably planned the event, but someone else carried out his instructions.'

Lestrade had been silently absorbing Holmes' explanation. Now he burst out. 'Are you saying, Mr Holmes, that all this was some kind of a joke? Do you mean no shot was fired and that me and my men have been wasting our time?'

'I do not think I would call it a joke, Lestrade. The major has never struck me as a man with much sense of humour, but it is certainly a ruse of some kind.'

Holmes reached into his pocket and tossed something across to the inspector. It was a small cylinder of coloured pasteboard, burned at one end – the remains of a small firework.

'A Guy Fawkes banger!' exclaimed Lestrade. 'I shall have my superiors make a stiff protest to the embassy!'

'Only to be told,' said Holmes, 'that the Russian ambassador cannot be held responsible for the actions of every prankster in London. Far better to let Kyriloff believe that you accept his story. That may lead us to discover what it is that really frightens the count.'

'What about,' I asked, 'the description which Kyriloff gave of the perpetrator? It sounded very much like—'

Holmes shot me a fiercely warning glance.

'—a complete invention,' I went on. 'Surely, such a man

would have been easily noticeable among the crowds in Rotten Row?'

'Certainly,' agreed Holmes, 'but he was not there. He was not even the man who ignited the firework.'

'How do you know, Mr Holmes?' asked Lestrade.

'Because young Freddy saw the man who was in the shrubbery and who left it just after the explosion. He was able not only to provide a very good description, but also to identify a picture.'

'A picture!' Lestrade exclaimed, open-mouthed. 'You have a picture of the perpetrator?'

Holmes reached into the inside pocket of his coat, withdrawing a folded sheet of paper.

'Not until young Freddy had given me a complete description of the man that he saw, and until I had formed a theory as to who that man might be, did I show him this picture. His response was immediate. "That," he said, "is the cove what lit the banger." He was completely sure.'

He passed the paper to the little detective, who sat and stared at it for some minutes.

'Might I ask, Mr Holmes,' said Lestrade eventually, 'who this picture represents and how you came by it?'

'As to who it represents, Lestrade, it is a picture of one of Major Kyriloff's aides, I suspect. It is certainly a young man who has been seen about a great deal in Kyriloff's company. I imagine that you will find him among the Intelligence operatives at the Russian Embassy. As to the picture's origin, that is a matter of confidentiality between myself and a client.'

Lestrade went to speak, but Holmes forestalled him with a raised palm.

'Before,' he said, 'you remind me that I could be arrested for obstructing the course of justice, I would say that my client has no idea of the name of that man, nor of his purposes. You would gain nothing by interviewing her.'

'Then I suppose I must accept what you say, Mr Holmes, but it's a pretty rum affair. If you're right, the Russians have faked an attack on one of their visitors to the Jubilee, but for what reason, Mr Holmes, for what reason?'

'I have told you what happened in Hyde Park today,

Lestrade. I rather think it is up to you to discover why it happened,' said Holmes, with a perfectly straight face.

The little inspector emptied his glass, thanked us for dinner and for Holmes' views on the case, and showed himself out.

When he had gone I turned to Holmes. 'Why,' I asked, 'did you not explain the business of the man in the striped blazer?'

Holmes lifted an eyebrow at me. 'Because, Watson, you and I know that no such person exists. It would be a shame to send poor Lestrade along a trail which will take him nowhere.'

Mrs Hudson tapped on the door and entered. 'While the inspector was here,' she said, 'this was delivered for you, Mr Holmes,' and she handed him a large brown envelope.

'Very good,' he said, and laid the packet down without opening it. Taking out his pocketbook he scribbled a few lines and gave the page to Mrs Hudson with some coins. 'Perhaps you will be so good,' he said, 'as to see that this message is sent as soon as the telegraph offices open.'

When she was gone he turned to me with a broad smile. 'Now, Watson,' he said, 'we seem to have discharged our obligations for the day. Would you object to a little music?'

When an investigation was frustrated, Holmes would vent his feelings on his violin, usually in a series of angry and dissonant phrases repeated indefinitely, but when in a good mood he was a delightful player with a considerable gift for improvisation. I made myself comfortable in my chair as he picked up his Stradivarius and launched into the first of a sequence of low, dreamy melodies. Soon the music had lulled me to sleep.

The brown envelope lay unopened on the table.

Eleven

A Visit to a Relative

Holmes and I were at breakfast next morning when the reply to his wire arrived. He slit the envelope, glanced briefly at its contents, and passed the form across the table to me with no comment. It said:

> MR SHERLOCK HOLMES, 221B BAKER STREET, LONDON.
> REGRET MR GREGORIEFF AND SISTER NO LONGER RESIDENT AT THIS ADDRESS OR IN MY EMPLOY. BELIEVE THEM TO BE RETURNING TO RUSSIA.
> AGATHA WORTLEY-SWAN

I passed it back when I had read it. 'Why did you wire the interpreter?' I asked.

'I merely wished to warn him not to use his eccentric disguise again, since a description had been given to Scotland Yard, and to seek an opportunity to talk to him. I also wished to warn him of what he was suspected before he read it in this morning's papers. In that I was evidently forestalled. He has already cut the slender thread which Scotland Yard might trace from him to Miss Wortley-Swan, which is a pity. It means we must pay a visit to Uncle.'

'Uncle?' I queried.

He nodded and set about applying marmalade to his toast. He was not, it seemed, going to elucidate. I tried another approach.

'Are you not in danger of seeking to assist the escape of a wanted man?' I asked.

'If Gregorieff were wanted for a crime he had actually committed, Watson, that might cause me some concern. As it is, he has, so far as I know, committed no crime in London except dressing outrageously. The crime for which Lestrade will seek him was not, as we know, Gregorieff's work. Lestrade may feel obliged by his official position to kowtow to the Russian Embassy. I certainly do not.'

Whereupon he turned to discussing various items that had caught his eye in the morning papers, including a short and garbled account of the alleged shooting in Hyde Park which included a description of the mysterious man in the striped blazer and bowler hat.

Breakfast done, Holmes invited me to accompany him on a visit to his uncle in the East End.

'You have an uncle in the East End?' I said, for I had never previously heard of such a relative. It was not impossible. I had known Sherlock Holmes for several years before he ever mentioned to me that he had an elder brother and that his brother was by way of being one of the most powerful men in the kingdom. I did not regard it as unlikely that there was another member of the family whom I had not previously met or heard of.

Holmes paused in walking out of the door and looked at me without expression. 'Everybody,' he said, 'has an uncle in the East End, Watson.'

Like so many of my friend's cryptic observations, it left me none the wiser, at least until our cab halted in a street near Jubilee Street and I saw the three gleaming brass balls of Saint Nicholas hanging outside a small shop.

'Ah!' I exclaimed. 'A pawnbroker! Uncle's!'

'Precisely, Watson,' was all my companion said as I followed him inside.

Inside, the shop was larger than its windows suggested, but most of the space was taken up with shelves and glass-fronted cabinets. It seemed that objects of every variety were displayed. There were racks of clothing, both men's and women's, in every style and condition from relatively shabby to almost brand-new; an entire case was full of mantelpiece clocks and another of pocket watches; a number of shelves displayed achievements of wax fruit under glass domes and cases with stuffed animals and birds; close to the ceiling, the gas lamps gleamed on the wondering glass eyes of an enormous stuffed white owl mounted on a perch.

There was only one customer at the counter as we entered, an enormously tall man with a broad back and a wide-brimmed hat which he held in one hand, revealing a thick head of greying hair.

'I'm sorry, Mr Poliakoff',' said the girl who stood behind the counter. 'I think you have seen everything we have in that line. Perhaps you should leave it a week or so and we can see what comes in.'

'Very well, my dear,' he said, turning from the counter. 'I will leave it awhile.'

Despite his gigantic size, his fiercely curled moustaches and wide beard, he nodded affably enough to Holmes and me as he passed us in the cluttered space of the shop and went to peruse the display cases behind us as Holmes stepped up to the counter.

'Can I help you, sir?' asked the pretty, oval-faced young woman who served in the shop. 'Were you wanting to leave something with us, or perhaps you were looking for something in particular.'

'I was looking,' said Holmes, 'for another of these. I wonder if you have one.'

He had taken an object from his coat pocket and now laid it on the marble countertop. I could see that it was a silver medallion attached to a brightly coloured ribbon, but I did not recognize it and I wondered what part in Holmes' scheme it played.

The young lady picked up the medal and examined it. 'I do not know,' she said, 'if we have one. I'm afraid that I know little of medals, but my father, he knows all about them. Let me ask if he will see you.'

She drew back a curtain behind her and stepped into a small hallway, calling, 'Father! There is a gentleman here about a medal. Will you see him?'

From somewhere a voice rumbled in what seemed to be a foreign language, and the young lady turned back to us.

74

Opening a hinged section of the counter, she showed us into the curtained hallway at the rear and pointed out a flight of stairs.

'My father's office is at the top,' she said, 'right opposite the stairs. The door will be open for you. I am sorry I cannot show you up, but I must not be away from the shop.'

We thanked her and climbed up the stairs to the top landing, where a pool of light was thrown from an open door. Inside, a plump, balding man with a small beard and neat moustache sat at a wide desk. He wore thick, small half-round spectacles, through which he was peering at an array of small jewellery set out on a black velvet cloth in front of him. He looked up as we entered and the lamplight flashed across his spectacles.

'Mr Holmes!' he exclaimed. 'Mr Holmes! What a pleasure! Come in, please, and you must be the Dr Watson who writes the stories about Mr Holmes. Be seated, gentlemen, be seated.'

He waved us both to chairs in front of his desk and wrapped away the jewellery in its cloth, slipping it into a desk drawer and turning a key on it.

When he had done, he adjusted his spectacles and looked from one to another of us. 'Now, gentlemen,' he said, 'how can I be of service to you? It is not, I take it, a medal that interests you?'

'The medal,' said Holmes, smiling, 'was, as always, in case you were not at your own counter. When last I called you had a young man here. Now I see you have an attractive young woman.'

'The young man? Ah, yes, he wanted to see the world. I told him stay here, I said, all the world passes through here sooner or later, but he must go. So now my daughter helps me. I have told her about the man with a strange medal, so that she knew what to do.'

It dawned on me that the medal was a device whereby Holmes could avoid hinting at his business with the pawnbroker in front of a customer or to the assistant. It occurred to me also that I had known Sherlock Holmes for most of twenty years, yet he could still surprise me by revealing another of the many contacts he had in all parts of the metropolis.

Holmes had reached into his pocket and produced what I recognized as the envelope delivered to him on the previous day. Its top had been slit and he withdrew from it two cards. When he laid them on the pawnbroker's desk I saw that they were both photographs, not of the clearest focus but both easily recognizable as the Russian interpreter, Gregorieff.

Our host moved a lamp, so that its light fell fully on the photographs, and bent over them. He looked at them silently for a minute or so.

'What is it that you wish to know, Mr Holmes?' he asked as he looked up.

'I wish to know anything at all about the man in those pictures,' said Holmes. 'I know what and who he claims to be, but I am certain that he has not told me all of the truth and maybe none of it.'

The old man nodded. 'I know him,' he said. 'I have done business with him, but perhaps what he tells me is no more true than what he tells you.'

'Perhaps not,' agreed Holmes, 'but others will have talked about him. You lend them money, you cash their cheques from home, you help them. They all talk to you. You are their friend. Even if this man has not told you the truth, someone will have given you a hint, some comment made, some remark dropped.'

The old man nodded again. 'What has he done wrong?' he asked.

'I do not know that he has done anything wrong,' said Holmes, 'but our friend Kyriloff at the embassy seems to be afraid of him for some reason.'

'Kyriloff? Afraid? Never! Kyriloff is not a man, he is a *golem*, made of clockwork and moved by the Devil. He cannot be afraid.'

'Then let us say that this man worries Kyriloff in some way. Kyriloff accuses this man of things which he did not do,' said Holmes and tapped a fingertip on the photographs.

'Then we must help him, Mr Holmes, we must help him. More than one that Kyriloff lies about has ended in prison and some have ended worse than that. This man,' and he tapped the picture in turn, 'is not a bomb-maker. He goes to the Social Democratic Federation meetings and he argues in their debates, but he is a voice of reason. Always he argues for democratic methods, not for revolution, not for the bomb and the gun.'

'Do you know his name and what he does for a living?' asked Holmes.

'He is called Gregori Gregorieff, so far as I know. He is a scholar who writes many languages and he used to make a small living from writing letters for people and helping them with documents. I know him because he sometimes brings people here to change their cheques or to pawn something. Then he started to work for an English lady.'

'Miss Wortley-Swan?' queried Holmes.

'That is the lady. He has brought her to my shop as well. They have come to redeem things for people that she was helping, or to buy clothing for them.'

'Do you know anything else about him?' pressed Holmes.

'Only what I have picked up from talking to Gregori himself and to his sister. Like so many hereabouts they were forced to leave Mother Russia because of something that happened to their family.'

'Have you any idea what that was?'

The old man lifted up both hands and shrugged his shoulders. 'Take your pick, Mr Holmes, take your pick. Flogging, imprisonment, rape, murder – these things have happened to many people here who come from Russia.' He shook his head sadly. 'No, I do not know what particular tragedy drove the Gregorieffs from home.'

'And where does he live?' asked my friend.

'There I can help you, Mr Holmes. In Barrow Street there is a lodging house. It has an old sign on the front saying "Murdock's Rents", but the man who keeps it is called Green. Gregorieff and his sister have lived there for some time now.'

Holmes stood up. 'I am grateful, Mr Goldstein, and I shall be more grateful if you will let me know of anything more you hear about the Gregorieffs, Kyriloff or Miss Wortley-Swan.'

'It is always a pleasure to see you, Mr Holmes, and a greater pleasure to assist you in your work.'

Holmes paused at the door. 'One more point,' he said. 'Have you ever heard of Count Stepan Skovinski-Rimkoff?'

'Ha!' snorted the pawnbroker. 'Have I heard of him? I tell you, Mr Holmes, if Kyriloff is a machine driven by the Devil, the count is one of the Devil's own beasts!'

'You have heard of him?' said Holmes.

'Nothing but evil I have heard. He is a cousin of the Tzar and he has great wealth and miles and miles of lands. There are many people here in London who have lived on his lands and who tell stories of him. He is a beast, Mr Holmes, a creature whose whole being is given to lust and cruelty!'

Twelve

An Encounter with the Tiger

'How long have you known the old man?' I asked Holmes as we made our way to Gregorieff's address.

'I have known Abram Goldstein more than twenty years,' replied Holmes. 'I met him when I was first setting up my practice in Montague Street. Even in those days, enquiries brought me quite often into these parts. I soon discovered that Mr Goldstein knew everything about his customers, his customers' neighbours, and their neighbours' neighbours. In addition, I was able to do him a favour or two and he did me one great one.'

'What was that?'

'He told me one day that he had seen a violin in a shop window near here that would be only a few shillings to buy. He also told me that he thought it was a Stradivarius, and he was right.'

Another question had puzzled me. 'Where,' I asked, 'did you come by the photographs of Gregorieff?'

He smiled. 'I simply asked Henry Cloke, the postcard photographer, to be near Miss Wortley-Swan's home yesterday morning. Equipped with all his paraphernalia he set himself up to make a view of that pretty lane where the lady lives. By chance, as it seemed, a small ragged boy accosted Gregorieff as he came out of the gate and kept him engaged long enough for Henry to obtain the photograph from which the portrait is an enlargement.'

I laughed. 'And of course the providential small boy will have been one of your Irregulars?'

'Of course,' he said.

We walked silently for a while and then Holmes pointed his stick across the street. 'There,' he said, and indicated a faded board with the words 'Murdock's Rents'.

It was one of those buildings of several storeys which may have been impressive when they were first built but which now are smoke-darkened and grim. Their tall, dark faces shadow the streets, so that the sun is only seen in the afternoon. Many of them have cheap shops on the ground floor and dozens of rooms above, let to as many lodgers as the owner can cram in. This one had the shop windows on its ground floor covered with boards, suggesting that the ground, too, was used for residence.

As we crossed the street towards our destination, I noticed that we had taken the attention of a man who was seated on the front steps of the house. Even at a little distance, there was no mistaking the great bulk and height, the wide beard and the fierce moustaches of the man Poliakoff whom we had seen in Goldstein's pawnshop. As soon as he had recognized us, he stood up and disappeared inside the building.

We made our way up the steps and into what was not, properly, an entry to the house. It was a narrow and unlit passageway that led from the street through to a fenced rear yard, but a side door in the passage gave access to the building's ground floor.

The grim building's dark interior spoke plainly of generations of poverty. The tall stairway was lit by one meagre gas jet, whose pale flame revealed worn boards underfoot and stair rails polished with the grease of dirty hands. The air was thick with the smell of stale cookery and unwashed bodies. Nobody was about as we entered, though sounds of movement could be heard above. It seemed our friend Poliakoff had disappeared somewhere within.

'Which floor?' I asked Holmes.

He shrugged his shoulders and stepped away into a corridor which seemed to run from front to back of the house. A couple of doors along it, a scrap of paper was pinned to a doorjamb. It turned out to be a business card which advertised:

Prof. GREGORIEFF,
of the University of St Petersburg,

TRANSLATOR & INTERPRETER
from and to
English, Russian, Polish, German,
French, Italian, Spanish and the
Scandinavian tongues.

Holmes knocked on the door and waited. While we waited, Holmes pointed with his stick at the crack beneath the door's edge, where what seemed to be the light of a candle flame flickered against the floor as though it was being moved about the room. There was no response and he knocked again. When there was still no answer, he tried the doorknob. It yielded and he stepped in. I followed him closely.

Although it was not one of the rooms whose windows were boarded, it was extremely dark inside, for the curtains were closed. Before my eyes could accustom themselves to the gloom, I was struck across the back of my head and flung across the room.

I awoke from unconsciousness to find myself huddled in a corner. Holmes stood beside me. The room was lit by only one candle, which had been placed on the mantelpiece. In front of the door through which we had come stood the man Poliakoff, appearing even more gigantic from my low viewpoint. Although his eyes were fixed on Holmes, he was holding a large revolver which was pointed steadily at me.

'Your friend is awake,' he said. 'So I tell you now. You make one move and I shoot your friend, then I shoot you.'

'I cannot see why,' said Holmes calmly. 'Our business is not with you. It is with Professor Gregorieff.'

'Gregorieff,' repeated the giant. 'What business do you have with Gregorieff? Are you English police or Kyriloff's spies? Eh?'

'We are not,' said Holmes, patiently, 'policemen or Kyriloff's spies. I am a consulting detective who has business with Professor Gregorieff. I mean him no harm and he may well be glad to hear what I have to say. Might I suggest that you call Gregorieff and ask him if he wishes to speak to me? He knows who I am.'

'If you knew Gregorieff,' said Poliakoff, 'you would know

where he lives, but you went to the old pawnbroker to find out. You are spies – police or Kyriloff's.'

My head was beginning to clear and I wondered whether it would be possible to take Poliakoff by the feet, but he stood far enough away to make it impossible. I had done my share on the rugby field, for my school and at Netley Hospital, and had been accounted useful at a low tackle, but I realized that he would have a bullet in me before I could reach him. Although his remarks were directed, it seemed, mainly at Holmes, his pistol pointed unwaveringly at me, and I knew that the slightest movement on my part might cause him to fire.

'We appear,' remarked Holmes, who seemed to have come to the same conclusion, 'to have reached a deadlock, Mr Poliakoff.'

'A deadlock? You think so?' said the giant. 'You think I cannot shoot you both?'

'Oh, I'm sure that you can,' agreed Holmes, 'but I am also sure that you are not so stupid. This is a populous area, my friend, and the sound of two pistol shots, even in this neighbourhood, will draw unwelcome attention.'

The comment had a certain amount of effect. Poliakoff's eyes shifted momentarily to the heavily curtained window, as though he wondered what lay outside, but his pistol remained pointed steadily at me.

'You think I need to shoot you?' he asked, and laughed a soft rumbling chuckle. 'I could break the pair of you at once with my bare hands. You know my name, but it means nothing to you. I am Nikolai Poliakoff, the unbeaten champion wrestler of Russia. I have beaten every contender from Vienna to Vladivostok. Do not think for one moment that I need a pistol to deal with you.'

Before Holmes could reply, footfalls sounded in the next room and the internal door behind Poliakoff opened.

I had already observed that Holmes had braced one leg, as though preparing for action. The sound of the door opening was sufficient. For a split second it diverted Poliakoff's attention, but it was enough.

As Poliakoff's eyes flicked towards the door, Holmes

stepped quickly away from me. Instantly the Russian's attention swung back, but instinctively he swung his weapon towards Holmes. In that tiny moment when the pistol was pointed at neither of us, my friend made his move. He stepped close up to the Russian giant and smashed the gun upwards with a blow of his forearm.

The wrestler swung his other arm as though to grapple Holmes in a bear hug, but Holmes was too fast for him. Still holding the Russian's right hand with the pistol high in the air, Holmes gripped his opponent's right elbow with his own right hand.

The Russian's left arm, which had been about to enclose Holmes' back, fell away. For a second or two they stood, locked and struggling, then my friend's features contorted as he found the point he sought in the crook of the wrestler's elbow, and applied the full force of his powerful fingers.

Despite the length and dexterity of my friend's fingers, they are the strongest I have ever seen on a man. I have watched Holmes use his bare hands to straighten a poker which the repellent Dr Grimesby Roylott* had doubled in two, so I have some idea of the pressure those long fingers can apply. As a doctor I had some idea of the damage and pain that he was inflicting by his grip on the Russian's arm.

A long strangled sound of pain escaped from the Russian wrestler's bearded lips and he lost his grip on the pistol, letting it fall to the floor. Now I came up from the floor, taking him behind the knees with all the force I could muster and any skill that I could remember.

It worked. Giving vent to what sounded like a spate of curses, the Russian toppled over and fell with Holmes on top of him, still relentlessly maintaining his grip on his opponent's elbow.

As soon as we hit the floor, I loosed the wrestler's ankles and cast about me for the pistol. It lay close to me and I snatched it up and scrambled to my feet, looking about me to see who had entered the room.

The intruder still stood in the opening of the internal door,

* See *The Speckled Band* by Sir Arthur Conan Doyle.

his face pale and his eyes wide at the sight of the violence his interruption had unleashed. It was the Russian translator.

'Nikolai! Nikolai!' he said. 'What are you doing? Leave these gentlemen alone, they have come to see me.'

With the presence of this new ally, Holmes felt able to release his grip on the gigantic wrestler, who pulled himself into a corner and slouched against the wall, rubbing his pained elbow and muttering.

Gregorieff advanced towards us as Holmes got up and straightened his dress. The Russian held out a hand to Holmes.

'Mr Holmes,' he said. 'I am so sorry that this has happened, but Nikolai is very protective of me and my sister. He evidently thought you were a danger to us.'

'He thought,' said Holmes, 'that we were policemen or Kyriloff's spies.'

Gregorieff looked down at Poliakoff and shook his head. 'I am astonished,' he said, 'that you subdued him. I have seen him fight many times, both in the wrestling ring and in situations of danger. I have never known anyone stop him before.'

Holmes smiled. 'The situation was one which my Japanese master would have called 'subduing the tiger', that is, reducing an armed opponent to helplessness, but it required your sudden arrival to distract him so that I could apply the grip. It is extremely painful but leaves no lasting harm. If he lifts nothing heavy with that arm for a day or two he will regain its use.'

Poliakoff had clambered to his feet and now joined us. He held out a hand. 'I am sorry,' he said, 'that I mistook you for Kyriloff's dogs. Excuse, please, my left hand, but I think I will be cautious with my right.'

'Perhaps,' said Gregorieff, 'you would both like tea while we discuss what brings you here?'

Thirteen

The Interpreter's Oath

Gregorieff led us into the adjacent room, evidently a sitting room for him and his sister. Unlike its neighbour, it was warm and clean, comfortably furnished and hung with attractive tapestries and prints.

Anna Gregorieff rose to greet us as we entered, and I was able to confirm the skill and accuracy with which Mrs Fordeland had sketched her. Soon we were all seated and Miss Gregorieff was pouring us black tea.

'Now, Mr Holmes,' said our host at last, 'I must apologize to you again for Nikolai's hastiness, but he fears for our safety.'

'So do I, Mr Gregorieff, so do I,' said Sherlock Holmes. 'That was one of my reasons for coming here today.'

'But how did you know I would be here?'

'Since I first observed you following Mrs Fordeland, and tracked you to your temporary place at Miss Wortley-Swan's, I have been aware that you must have another place in London, somewhere you could change from Gregori Gregorieff, interpreter, to the somewhat eccentric character who followed Mrs Fordeland. Where else but among your countrymen in the East End?'

'And you came to warn me of something, Mr Holmes?'

'I rather think you are already aware of any warning I can give,' said Holmes. 'This morning I had a telegram from Miss Wortley-Swan, informing me that you had left for Russia. Evidently you left her home before the newspapers carried the story of events in Hyde Park yesterday.'

Gregorieff nodded. 'I was warned by a friend in the embassy, that the police would be looking for me at Kyriloff's behest.

85

I thought it better to leave a dead end at Miss Wortley-Swan's. They might trace me there, as you did, but I hoped that they would not trace me further.'

'Nor will they,' said Holmes, 'provided that you are careful. Major Kyriloff wants the Metropolitan Police to hunt for you, but I have explained to Scotland Yard what really happened in Hyde Park, so they will not be in any great hurry. Even were you to be so unlucky as to be arrested for that matter, I can point you to two witnesses who know that you were only just emerging from Miss Wortley-Swan's gate in Sussex at about the time of the so-called attempt on Count Stepan.'

'Witnesses!' exclaimed Gregorieff and his sister, simultaneously.

'As you left your lodgings yesterday morning, were you not stopped by a small and importunate boy with a tale of hardship?'

'That's right,' said the Russian. 'He was a poor ragged child and he asked for money. I gave him some pennies, but I also told him that it was below the dignity of a working man to beg for subsistence. But how did you know this, Mr Holmes?'

'Because,' said Holmes, 'the lad was sent by me. After we met, it seemed to me that I must pursue some enquiries about you, and it occurred to me that a photograph would be useful.'

The Russian looked upset. 'Why should you wish to pursue enquiries about me, Mr Holmes? I have done nothing wrong.'

'So far as I know, you have not,' agreed Holmes. 'But you have done certain things that strike me as singular, and I formed the impression when we met at Miss Wortley-Swan's that your answers may have been strictly true, but they were not entirely helpful. I have come here today in the hope that you may feel able to give me more informative answers and also to tell you what really happened in Hyde Park yesterday.'

The interpreter was wary. 'What did occur in Hyde Park yesterday?' he asked. 'The newspapers say that a shot was fired at Count Skovinsky-Rimkoff, which did not injure him. They say the intending assassin got away. You know differently?'

'I know that no shot was fired in Hyde Park, Professor. A

farthing firework was detonated in the shrubbery alongside Rotten Row as Count Stepan and Major Kyriloff rode there. Major Kyriloff insists that it was a pistol shot, fired by a bearded man in a striped blazer and bowler hat. As you know, it was not. The firework was detonated by one of Kyriloff's own minions.'

'How come you know so much about this matter?' asked the Russian.

'Because Scotland Yard consulted me and, as is my practice, I examined the evidence and spoke to the only reliable, observant, witness. That led me to the conclusions which I have outlined to you. It also led me to certain other conclusions which I have not passed on to Scotland Yard.'

'Which are?' queried our host.

'Firstly, that the entire episode was staged as an excuse to ask Scotland Yard to hunt for you; secondly, that Kyriloff does not know who you really are, or he would have sought you out himself; and thirdly, that something about you is gravely threatening to Count Stepan.'

The Russian sat silent.

'You do not,' said Holmes, 'demur from my conclusions, so I take it that they are accurate. That being the case, you might expect to be in danger from Scotland Yard as well as Kyriloff. At present you are not. Scotland Yard now knows that yesterday's incident was a device of Kyriloff's and Kyriloff does not know who you really are. If that should change, you will be in grave danger. You do not need my opinion that Kyriloff is ruthless.'

The Russian nodded again. 'Mr Holmes,' he said, 'please do not think that I am not grateful that you have made Scotland Yard aware of Kyriloff's trick and that you have not revealed my identity to them. Nevertheless, there are reasons why I may not be able to answer your questions.'

'If you will permit me,' said Holmes, 'I shall ask them. I have no means of compelling you to answer them, nor even to answer them truthfully, but I believe that you will not be deliberately dishonest.'

He gazed questioningly at Gregorieff, who said, 'I will answer what I can, Mr Holmes.'

'Splendid!' exclaimed my friend. 'Perhaps you could begin by explaining your connection to Mrs Diana Fordeland.'

Glances were exchanged between the brother and sister, then Gegorieff said, 'I worked for her as an interpreter many years ago, when she visited Russia for a magazine.'

'And you have not met since?' asked Holmes.

The Russian shook his head.

'You have not remained in communication with the lady?'

Again the Russian shook his head.

'When did you first become aware that she was in London, Professor?'

'Only days ago. I had heard that she had left England long ago. I was astounded to see her in London.'

'But you made no attempt to contact her?'

'Certainly not, Mr Holmes. It would have been a breach of my word, a failure of honour!'

'And why might that be?' asked Holmes, quietly.

Again Gregorieff glanced at his sister. 'The last time that Mrs Fordeland and I spoke it was in Vladivostok, before she sailed for Japan, at the end of her tour across Russia. On that occasion we both agreed that it would be better if we never contacted each other. I have never sought to do so and she has never contacted me. It was the merest unhappy chance that I discovered that she was in London. I still do not know why.'

Holmes looked at the interpreter with a thoughtful expression. 'Mrs Fordeland,' he said at last, 'is in London on her way to the continent with her granddaughter. She has also been invited to meet King Chula of Mongkuria, whose governess she was many years ago. His Highness is a guest of Queen Victoria at the Jubilee celebrations. So far as I know, there is no other reason, no ulterior motive, for the lady's presence in London, unless, of course, you can enlighten me.'

Gregorieff shook his head vigorously. 'No, no,' he said. 'I am sure you are right.'

'Then,' said Sherlock Holmes, 'if, as you say, there is a pact between you and Mrs Fordeland by which you have agreed not to contact each other, may I ask what is your purpose in following the lady about England, dressed in such a manner that your presence was bound to be remarked?'

'I was in disguise.'

'Ha!' snorted Holmes. 'You were disguised as one might seek to disguise an elephant by painting stripes upon it! I grant you that Mrs Fordeland did not recognize you behind the false beard and padding, but she was bound to become aware that she was followed.'

'The disguise was so that Mrs Fordeland should not recognize me, but so that Major Kyriloff and his man could not fail to observe that they were followed.'

Holmes widened both eyes. 'So you were not, in fact, pursuing Mrs Fordeland, but Kyriloff and his henchman? Extraordinary! May I ask why?'

Gregorieff shifted uncomfortably in his seat. 'Because,' he said, 'when I became aware that the lady was in London, I was already aware that Count Skovinski-Rimkoff was here. I was afraid that he would discover Mrs Fordeland's presence – as indeed he did – and that his discovery might place her in danger.'

He closed his mouth at the end of that answer with a finality which suggested that he would vouchsafe no more information. Nevertheless, after considering the answer for a moment, Sherlock Holmes pressed on.

'What led you to believe,' he asked, 'that the presence of both Count Skovinski-Rimkoff and Mrs Fordeland in London at the same time placed the lady in danger?'

Gregorieff cast about him as though seeking a way of escape. When, at last, he answered, it was in a tone which was almost an entreaty.

'I cannot tell you more, Mr Holmes. It is a matter of honour. It is a question of an oath given to Mrs Fordeland – given for her protection. I know that you are acting in her interest and at her request, Mr Holmes, but it is she and not I who must reveal these matters to you. She will not do so unless you assure her that she has my agreement to her telling you. Then, perhaps, you will understand this affair and the danger which the count poses.'

Once again Holmes regarded the professor thoughtfully. Then he rose and picked up his stick.

'Very well,' he said. 'I shall pursue the matter with my

client. In the meantime I will put two last questions. The first is whether your oath to Mrs Fordeland arises out of any romantic attachment of the lady—'

'Certainly not, Mr Holmes. Certainly not,' interrupted the Russian. 'It is far more important than that.'

'—and the second,' continued Holmes, 'is whether your connection with Miss Wortley-Swan has anything to do with Mrs Fordeland?'

Gregorieff looked relieved. 'Most definitely not,' he said, firmly. 'It is as I have said, that Miss Wortley-Swan employs me about her business. That is all.'

'I believe,' said Holmes, 'that you have told me the truth, though evidently not all of it. I hope, for your sake, that you have withheld nothing that may damage my client's interest.'

'Mrs Fordeland,' said Gregorieff, 'is a brave and intelligent lady for whom I have nothing but the highest admiration. Please believe me, Mr Holmes, when I say that I would do nothing to harm the lady.'

We thanked the brother and sister for their hospitality and took our leave.

Fourteen

A Time for Questions

I admit freely that Holmes' conversation had left me entirely confused, and I remarked as much to him in our cab on the way back to Baker Street. He merely nodded.

'What do you make of it, Holmes?' I persisted.

'I, Watson, make nothing of it. The data is insufficient. At the present state of our knowledge it would be possible to create six or seven theories which would meet the facts, but none of them, I suspect, would be the right one. It is very Russian.'

'Very Russian?'

'Indeed. I was thinking, Watson, of a particular type of Russian doll, I think that they are called *matrioshki*. The thing is made of turned wood and designed to stand on its base, painted to represent a jolly old peasant woman. It will unscrew in the middle, and inside it is a slightly smaller but similar figure, which also unscrews in the middle, and so on until you have a long line of little wooden ladies of descending size.'

'I don't quite see the comparison with the present case,' I said.

'Our *matrioshka*, Watson, works in reverse. We start from what seems to be a relatively straightforward problem and as soon as we begin to interest ourselves we discover within it the interest of the Russian Embassy and the curious behaviour of two other Russians. No sooner do we track down the mysterious man in a beard than Kyriloff sets his silly plot in Hyde Park. Now Gregorieff tells us that his employment by Miss Wortley-Swan has no connection with Mrs Fordeland. Each of our discoveries gets larger, not smaller.'

'Do you believe him, Holmes?'

'He has all the hallmarks of a man who is telling the truth.'

'You don't think that he's merely another bomb-throwing lunatic?' I said.

'No,' said Holmes. 'In that respect I would stand by the opinion of old Goldstein. He is a most perceptive man and has never led me astray.'

But there were a bunch of fellows tried in the Black Country while you were away, Holmes. They were making bombs to send to Russia and they seemed to be a completely ordinary group. There was a railway booking clerk, a cobbler, an engine driver and I don't know what, but they were making bombs for use in Russia.'

Holmes smiled. 'I sometimes find it difficult to grasp your logic, Watson. If I understand you, you are saying that the conviction of a group of British working men for making bombs in Britain to be used in Russia makes it more likely that the purpose of a Russian radical in London is to throw bombs in London? Is that your argument?'

'You can always defeat me in argument, Holmes, you know that,' I said, huffily.

'You defeat yourself, old friend, by failing to apply logic. There is no indication whatsoever that Gregorieff is a bomber or an intending bomber, so his situation has no connection with the events to which you refer. Added to which, you seem to have taken a little too much notice of the press reports of the case and failed to consider that journalists invent things in order to sell newspapers, while police officers invent things in order to obtain convictions.'

'The ringleader confessed,' I stated.

'You may have the advantage of me, Watson. I was out of the country at the time, but I have read something of the case since my return. Was not that "confession" made by a man who had been kept on bread and water for weeks and then fed whisky in the middle of the night?

'I seem to recollect,' continued Holmes, 'that the chief constable freely admitted dosing the poor fellow with spirits, saying that he thought it might make him more amenable. Evidently it did.'

'But wasn't there a fellow mixed up in that who said he was a professor of languages?' I persisted.

'You are, I believe, remembering a man called Auguste Coulon. Certainly he claimed to be a professor of languages, Watson, but there are many, and I am among them, who believe that he was a spy for the authorities and may have been an agent provocateur. The anarchists at the Autonomie Club believed him so and flung him out. If your peculiar logic is about to suggest that, because Coulon was a professor of languages and was involved with anarchists, so is Gregorieff, then I might remind you that old Goldstein told us that Gregorieff frequented the Anarchist and Socialist meetings at the Working Men's Club, stating firmly that the Russian is a voice of reason in their often heated debates. No, Watson, the mere similarity of profession and association with anarchists fails to convince me that Gregorieff is either spy or bomb-thrower.'

'So, what will you do next?' I asked, in an effort to change the topic.

'Next,' said Holmes, 'I shall stop at a Post Office and wire Mrs Fordeland to meet us at Baker Street tomorrow. Perhaps, when she is there, she will have the goodness to tell us what this is all about. Always, of course, assuming that she knows.'

In the many years that I shared a home with my friend and accompanied him on his enquiries and adventures, I never learned to predict accurately his changes of mood. I was afraid that Gregorieff's refusal to answer questions would plunge Sherlock Holmes into one of his finger-drumming moods of frustration, but once his telegram was sent he seemed to forget the whole business of his investigation and demonstrated once again his astonishingly wide knowledge of curious and entertaining subjects.

I had expected that Mrs Fordeland might be with us early on the next day and so remarked to Holmes when she did not appear.

'I would have thought that she would be anxious to learn what progress you have made,' I said.

He smiled. 'I put sufficient into my wire to suggest to Mrs

Fordeland that I will have further questions for her. She is not, I think, an impulsive person, and I imagine she is spending some little time considering whether she can answer any more questions, whether she should do so and, if so, in what manner.'

It was, in fact, after Holmes and I had finished luncheon that Mrs Hudson announced our client. She was dressed as before, simply but elegantly, and with that slight touch of decoration that betrayed her artistic personality, and she seemed, if anything, more nervous than on our first meeting. Holmes offered her the basket chair and had tea served.

When we were settled, Holmes leaned over and took from his desk the envelope that contained the photographs of Gregorieff.

'Mrs Fordeland,' he said, keeping the envelope in his hands, 'will you tell me what you know of Miss Agatha Wortley-Swan?'

She looked puzzled. 'Is that not,' she said, 'the name of a lady whom you have mentioned to me before? Aside from that, I know nothing of her. I have never knowingly met her and have, so far as I know, no connection with her.'

Holmes nodded. 'Nevertheless,' he said, 'there is a connection between you.' He slid the photographs from their envelope and laid them on the table in front of our guest. 'This man is the connection,' he said.

Mrs Fordeland leaned forward to examine the pictures, then started back, her mouth agape. 'This is . . . this is Gregori Gregorieff. He is older here, but it is him. He was my interpreter, years ago in Russia. Where did you come by these pictures, Mr Holmes?'

'I had them taken, two days ago, in a village in Sussex,' he replied.

Again she reacted with astonishment. 'He is here? In England? Now?'

Holmes nodded. 'Not only is he in England, he is in London and only minutes away from us. Does it surprise you to learn that he is the man who was following you about hidden behind a large false beard?'

Now her astonishment silenced her. She simply sat and shook her head in bewilderment while Holmes watched her.

'I have questioned Professor Gregorieff,' said Holmes after a moment, 'and you may be pleased to hear that he has steadfastly refused to answer any question that might reveal the nature of the secret that lies between you. He has told me that the two of you entered into a pact in Vladivostok, whereby neither of you would ever reveal what is known to both of you. Is that correct, Mrs Fordeland?'

There was a long silence, during which the lady picked up the photographs and turned them in her hands. 'That is correct, Mr Holmes,' she said at last. 'We made such an agreement. All I can or will tell you is that there was nothing wrong in our agreement. It was made to protect each other and other people.'

'I believe you,' said Holmes. 'But you can, if you will, tell me more, for Professor Gregorieff has given me a message for you. He has asked me to tell you that, if you wish to reveal the subject of your secret pact, you may do so.'

There was another long silence while she looked at the table. At last she lifted her eyes to my friend's. 'You must be telling the truth, Mr Holmes, because none but Gregori and I have ever known of that agreement before. He is right. The time has come to tell you what I had hoped to avoid. Do you think I might have some more tea?'

Fifteen

A Time for Answers

The tea was served and we took it in silence. Our client drank with her eyes lowered.

When she had finished her tea she stood up and walked to the window, where she remained for several minutes, looking down into the street. Holmes' eyes never left her but he made no sound.

At last she turned about and spoke, though she remained standing at the window, perhaps because its sunlit background made it difficult for us to see her expression.

'I had hoped,' she said, with a clear and firm intonation, 'that what has taken place in London had nothing to do with my past, but you have proved to me, Mr Holmes, that it does. For that reason, it would be unfair to you were I not to reveal the matter that lies between myself and Professor Gregorieff. To explain that, I must also reveal certain other things which are not the subject of my promise to the professor, merely the subject of a long-held vow to myself.'

She paused and we remained silent.

At last she said, 'Dr Watson, you have told me that you have read my first book. Leaving aside anything that you may have learned since I came to consult Mr Holmes, will you tell me what you know of my past from reading that book?'

I shifted in my seat. It was a good many years since I had read her account of her years in Mongkuria, but it had made a memorable impression upon me.

'I believe,' I said, 'that you are British by birth, the daughter of a Welsh officer in the army. That you married another officer, that you have a child or children by him, but that he

96

died unfortunately in the Malay States. Widowed, and with no great fortune, you took up teaching to support yourself and your children and, through a friend in the Consular Service, became aware that the King of Mongkuria was seeking an English governess for his many children. With considerable courage, if I may say so, you applied for and were accepted in that appointment.'

She nodded slowly.

'Would you be surprised,' she asked, 'to know that what you believe is untrue?'

I was confused. 'I really cannot say,' I replied. 'I have always believed those to be the bald facts of your life.'

She nodded again.

'I was not,' she said, 'the daughter of a Welsh officer. I was one of two daughters of a Welsh private soldier, born at Ahmednugger in India. My mother was a woman of mixed blood. You, Doctor, have served in the East. You will be able to imagine, as perhaps Mr Holmes cannot, the conditions of squalor and poverty in which I grew.'

It was my turn to nod, and to cast my mind back to the other ranks' quarters to which my medical duties had sometimes taken me. I remembered the great, dirty common living quarters of the squaddies, with a corner set aside and separated by matting screens to provide a little privacy for married soldiers. Behind them was little room to live and move. The bed was provided for a soldier, which he might share with his wife or paramour. Children could sleep only on mats laid on the floor beneath the bed. Sometimes, when duty kept soldiers away from the barrack room, male children were allowed to occupy the empty beds, but this privilege was never given to girls. Our client and her sister would have grown up sleeping under their parents' bed. The first time that ever I saw such an arrangement I was deeply angry at the contempt with which our Empire treated those who defended its frontiers and their unfortunate children. In addition, the family would be surrounded by the common barrack room where the private soldiers ate, drank and pursued their amusements. I thought of my own dear Mary, herself an officer's daughter and so like our client in many ways. It was difficult to imagine this

97

poised, intelligent, educated and resourceful lady emerging from such squalor and moral peril.

'I see,' continued Mrs Fordeland, 'from your expression, that you know the circumstances to which I refer. That I do so is because it is relevant to who I am and to what occurred in Russia. I will not dwell on the physical conditions in which I lived with my poor mother and sister. My father died before my birth and my mother, for economic reasons if no other, rapidly married another private soldier. Private soldiers were not then and are not now well paid. My mother had to take in laundry from single soldiers to make ends meet, and Eliza and I had to help her with this drudgery. In England such a life would be a burden; in the heat and dust of India it was akin to slavery.'

She paused and stepped to the table, pouring herself another cup of tea and retaking her seat in the basket chair.

'There was no future for us,' she went on, 'except to be evicted from the barracks at fifteen. Where might we then go? A small requirement existed for maids for officers' households, but very few, for the majority were plentifully staffed with cheap Indian labour, and few ladies would care to have about their house and in contact with their children what they called a 'barrack rat'. We were regarded as inevitably corrupted by the life in which we were bred, and it is sad to say that many of us were. No English merchant or trader in the town would employ a girl. Our only future lay in marrying another private soldier and repeating the heritage of misery.'

She sipped her tea and lifted her eyes to ours. 'At an early age,' she declared, 'I determined that I would not submit to such a cycle. I realized that education was the only chance that I had. The garrison school was not the best, but it had books and it had teachers, and to those two lanterns I clung with desperation that they would guide me out of my wretched existence. Every minute which I spent in school was not only a minute away from the squalor and drudgery of the barrack room, it was an investment in escape.'

A small smile lit up her sombre expression. 'There was another source of light in my life, gentlemen. As I grew, I became aware of a young clerk in the barracks, Rupert Eland.

He was only a few years older than I, and we became fast friends. He became the greatest light in my young life, because a marriage to him, when he was of sufficient standing and income to take a wife, would solve all my problems in an instant.'

She shook her head. 'But it was not, it seemed, to be. I was fourteen, rising fifteen and soon to be forbidden to live in the barracks, when my stepfather took a hand. He was not going to risk having a daughter living beyond the barracks, one that he would have to support, and so he commenced arrangements for me to marry one of his fellows, another private soldier. I could not wait for Rupert's advancement, for the grim future which I feared was almost upon me.'

She set her jaw and looked directly at us, as though daring us to query what she was about to say.

'I ran away,' she said. 'I lied about my age and background and attached myself to the retinue of an English missionary who was departing for Singapore. The teaching which I had absorbed in the garrison classroom I turned to account in the mission. In the years that followed I became a good teacher and acquired a knowledge of the world at large, and of the Orient in particular, which has been vouchsafed to few women, along with a wide range of oriental languages.'

The smile returned to her face. 'But I never forgot my Rupert,' she said. 'After a few years I returned to India. My poor mother had aged and grown more worn, but my wretched stepfather had changed not at all. He still believed that I would marry some uncouth private of his choice. I was now of an age to make my own decisions as to matrimony, and I did so. I married Rupert Eland, though he had changed his name to Fordeland.'

The smile broadened. 'It is, I expect, difficult for men such as yourselves to imagine what marriage meant to me. The life of a junior officer's wife is not a paradise, but it was so far from the squalor in which I had been raised that it might well have been. A junior officer's wife still lives a life that is bound by service to the army and the Empire, but the differences were, for me, enormous. To occupy our own premises, to employ our own servants, to have space and time to pursue my artistic and intellectual interests, to be able to meet with other ladies who shared my interests, to share my life with a man whom I loved and admired, was as much as I could have desired.'

She became thoughtful again and sipped her tea. 'Of course, we travelled, we followed where the Empire required Rupert. We travelled in the East, we were in Australia and we went to Singapore. During that time I bore Rupert two children, a boy and a girl. Some might think that our life was hard, but I do not. I did not wish for more.'

She gazed past us, looking out of the window, and perhaps she saw those far-off days in the Orient.

'It ended in a cruel misfortune,' she continued. 'Rupert had joined some brother officers on a tiger-hunting expedition. I was anxious that he return by nightfall, partly because I was aware that young officers in a hunting camp fall into ways of which I did not approve. I urged him to return at the end of the day and he promised to do so. He kept his promise, as I knew he would. Although he had lingered in camp after their hunt, he rode hard to reach home before sundown.'

She hesitated, as though to nerve herself for the recollection and recitation.

'He had barely arrived home,' she said, 'when he collapsed. We put him to bed, but there was nothing to be done. He died from heatstroke.'

Holmes allowed the silence to stretch a while, but eventually I said quietly, 'It must have been a calamity for you, Mrs Fordeland.'

'It was,' she said. 'It was. Rupert had always been my future and had become the mainstay and centrepost of my life. At one blow I had lost my only love and the support of our little family. Rupert had not been one of those gilded young men who adopt the army as a gentlemanly occupation until they inherit family wealth. He had no prospect of family wealth, no independent income. He was a career soldier. I had no home to which I might retreat, neither in India nor in England.'

She set her jaw again. 'It was up to me to ensure that my children and I survived. The only skill that I possessed was in teaching, so I set up a school for the children of officers.

It barely paid the way, but it kept my children and me from absolute penury. Nevertheless, I was always aware that our situation was precarious and that I must take steps to ensure a better future for my children. So it was that, when a friend in the consulate told me of the King of Mongkuria's search for an English governess, I applied for and was accepted in the post.'

She drew a long breath, as though an awkward task had been completed.

'You have read my account of my years in Mongkuria, Dr Watson,' she said. 'I assure you that I did not alter that part of my story. King Chula has said that I 'made up from my imagination what was deficient in my memory', but that is not so; It is as true as my observation, my recollection and my pen could make it, so I shall not take up your time by reciting it all again. You may wonder why I have told you so much of my past, but it seems to me that you should understand fully how I came to be what I am and what I was when I visited Russia. It may assist you in understanding my reaction to what happened there.'

Sixteen

A Journey Through Russia

'It had always been my intention to return to Mongkuria. Indeed, it had taken me no little time to persuade the King to grant me leave to come to England to visit my daughter. Unfortunately, while I was here, the King died suddenly. His son was only fifteen years old, so a regency ensued, and they did not invite me to return.'

She looked at both of us, who had sat silent through this recitation.

'I will not bore you with details of what is, essentially, family history,' she said. 'My daughter's marriage eventually ensured that we made our home across the Atlantic. However, I was not prepared to be simply an ageing pensioner of my wealthy son-in-law. My books had been received with no little success, and I established an income from writing and lecturing, largely, I may say, on the reduced status of women in all parts of the world. It was that which brought me to the attention of an American magazine editor and led to the offer to travel through Russia.'

Once more she paused and looked out of the window.

'It seemed to be,' she said, 'a wonderful opportunity. So much is said and written about Russia by people who have never been there, and so much by people who have their own secret motives for what they say. I was being given the chance to travel the Tzar's kingdom from end to end and to report on it as freely as I wished. It should have been the chance of a lifetime, and of course I saw it as such and jumped at it.'

She looked back to us, and continued, in what struck me as a reflective tone.

'I was the first Western woman, if not the first Western

journalist, to traverse the whole length of Russia. My articles were a resounding success in the States and in Canada. The company that commissioned my trip was so pleased that they offered me an editor's post. I turned them down. You may wonder at that, as you may wonder that I never wrote a book about my experiences in Russia, but I turned down the offer of employment and I never wrote a book about Russia, because there were things which I wished never to recall and things which I had promised never to say.'

She braced her shoulders and a brisker tone entered her voice.

'Russia,' she said, 'was everything I thought it might be and many things which I had not imagined. Have either of you been there?'

We both nodded.

'Then, perhaps, you will not need me to tell you of the splendours which the great cities of Russia display. London, Paris, New York, Vienna, all have their fame for the richness and quality of their society and their entertainments, but Moscow and Saint Petersburg are close to their match. I saw performances, I attended receptions, which might have been in any of the world's great cities. I did not actually meet the then Tzar and Tzarina, but more than once I was at receptions which they attended. Of the social, artistic and intellectual life of the country I soon had no doubt, but that was not what I had gone to Russia to see.

'I was there,' she said, 'to see as much of the real Russia as I might, for the great cities are no more representative of Russia than London is of all England or New York of all America. Nevertheless, it was in the cities that I began first to see the shadowed side of Russian society. In the manufactories which were already beginning to spread and expand in those days, I saw the way in which men, and women, were forced to toil and the hardships which they had to bear. I am not unworldly, gentlemen. I pride myself that I know more of the realities of life than many of my sex. I know that life in the West End of London is separated from life in the East End by a great social and economic gulf, and I know that this circumstance pertains, on a greater or lesser scale, in every city everywhere in the world.

'But I was not there to see just their great cities. As we travelled eastwards, I saw more of their smaller cities, their country towns, their villages. Wherever I went I tried to see things as they really were, and not as officials might like me to see them. I was present at feasts and funerals and even a birth. More and more I became aware that poverty and fear are the lot of millions of workers in Russia. In the country, perhaps even more so than in the cities, they live lives which no Briton would stand. In the cities there are signs of unrest, but any association which is deemed to be involved in any kind of politics is put down harshly and its leaders sent to prison or banished to Siberia. In the country they dare not even try. They live in fear of the whim of their landowners, who have absolute power over them.'

'But I thought the system of serfdom had been abolished?' I said.

'So it has, Doctor, so it has. But it makes little difference. If you come of a former serf family, you may not leave your village without the permission of the village council. If you have land and wish to buy more or to improve what you have, you may not borrow money to do so unless the village council is prepared to guarantee your credit, which often they are not prepared to do. Serfdom has been abolished in name only.'

She had become more and more animated as she described the plight of Russia's people.

'You seem to have been deeply affected by what you saw,' I commented.

'I told you much of my own background – more than I have revealed to others – so that you should understand the impact which my journey through Russia made upon me. I have seen poverty and misery in many parts of the world, gentlemen, but in most places – even in our snobbish old England – a poor man or woman may keep some pride and some hope. In Russia that is impossible. Its people live like farm animals, kept always under the eye, and often literally under the lash, of their lords.'

'It sounds like the Middle Ages!' I exclaimed.

'That is exactly what it is like,' she said. 'Imagine a land as wide as or wider than America or Australia, with all the resources of such a land in agriculture and mineral wealth, with magnificent cities and a glittering upper society, and imagine that such a land has not advanced from medieval thoughts and systems. That is Russia.'

'And you are sure,' asked Holmes, 'that the impression you brought back is the correct one?'

'It cannot be other, Mr Holmes. It rests not only upon what I saw, but upon what many people described to me. In addition, I had the assistance of Professor Gregorieff. He was only a student then, but he was already considerably skilled in Russian dialects and several continental languages. He was recommended to me as an interpreter, and he proved invaluable to me, not merely in assisting my journey and in making communication with the natives easier, but he has a very wide knowledge of his own country and was often able to confirm that what I had hoped might be some local aberration was, sadly, a widespread practice. Once he had joined me I found him so useful that I kept him with me all the way to Vladivostok. I could not know what it would mean.'

She gave no explanation of this comment. Instead she went on to describe the cumbersome lethargy of Russian administration and the many small difficulties which she had met on her journey. Like many countries which have a widespread and inefficient bureaucracy, it appears that often the only way to make progress was by bribery, and it appeared that Gregorieff had been adept at knowing exactly whom should be bribed and with how much.

'I could, I suppose, have taken a carriage on the railway and kept it all the way across to Vladivostok, but it was my intention to discharge my commission properly, so we made many stops, sometimes for a day or two. This necessitated waiting for trains, which were frequently late, not by minutes, but sometimes by hours or even half a day. Mostly we travelled by larger trains, which compare very favourably with those in which I have crossed Australia, America and Canada, but sometimes my agenda or the vagaries of the railroad system necessitated using rackety little trains which shuttled along, stopping at every tiny village.

'We had, despite these difficulties and our many stops,

made a great distance into Russia and must have been nearly halfway across its entire length. Gregori had made clear that the train on which we were then travelling would stop at a number of small towns, virtually indistinguishable from many that we had visited. As a result I was looking forward to a fairly long, uninterrupted passage, during which I might catch up with my writing. We had a large and comfortable apartment on the train, with a sitting room and even its own kitchen, and Gregori told me that he had taken on a Russian woman to see to my comforts, so that I might get the maximum benefit from this part of our journey.'

She drew a long breath before continuing.

'We had boarded that train in the late morning. All afternoon we traversed wild and lonely country, high moorland and forest. Only very occasionally did I see any sign of habitation near the track. Gregori's Russian woman had boarded with us, but kept herself to the kitchen. She served meals in my sitting room, but it appeared that she had no English, and my Russian, though I worked on it at every opportunity, was not sufficient to exchange more than the simplest courtesies with her. Nevertheless, she kept us well fed and, by nightfall, I was enjoying the peace of this interlude in my crowded and erratic progress across Russia.

'Dark had fallen and Gregori and I were discussing certain items about which I intended to write, when our train came to a sudden and violent halt. After the squeal of the train's brakes being deployed and above the sound of steam venting, I thought that I detected cries and what sounded like shots from the darkness outside the train. I knew of no banditti in Russia who waylaid trains as they still do in the United States, and I exclaimed in alarm.

'Gregori jumped from his seat, looking thoroughly alarmed himself. "Stay here," he said. "I will go and see what this is about. Do not leave your compartment."

'"But who would stop the train?" I asked. "Only the authorities, I think, but I do not know why. Let me go and find out," he replied and with that he left the compartment.'

Seventeen

An Incident at Night

'I was not, at first, frightened. I think I was more annoyed that our train had been delayed once more. I assured myself that holding up trains is an American habit, not a Russian one, and that the sounds which I took to be shots were probably fired in exuberance.'

She drew another deep breath and stared at the table top.

'I remained in that state of happy ignorance for a few minutes. Then I heard again what I imagined to be shots from outside. I parted the curtains of my compartment and peered out into the night. At first I could see nothing, because of the light from my compartment, but I lowered the gas lamps and looked again. Close to the railway line there seemed to be a group of mounted men, who were milling about, emitting occasional cries. The sounds which I had taken to be shots were, in fact, the crack of whips.

'I still did not perceive any real danger. These men seemed to be drunk and noisy, and though I thought that I saw rifles slung at their saddles, there appeared to be no hostile intent.

'I had watched them for a minute or two, more in curiosity than trepidation, when the compartment door opened and Gregori returned. He was white-faced and evidently deeply disturbed. "What is happening?" I asked him. He was so distressed that he began to answer me in Russian and had to begin again. "It is the local landowner. He has stopped the train." "Why on earth would he do that?" I asked. Gregori was so upset that he stammered. "There is – there is – someone – a young woman, a girl, that they think is on the train. She was employed on the estate here and has run away. He has come with his men to take her back. They are searching the train for her. You must give me your passport and travel papers. I will try to stop them searching here."'

The muscles of our client's face tightened at the recollection.

'I was outraged,' she said. 'I told Gregori, "But serfdom is ended. Why should she not go if she does not wish to stay?" He looked at me helplessly. "It makes no matter," he said. "Out here in the country, the landowners own the people as well. You must give me your papers."

'He was evidently deeply frightened and worried, so I put my passport and travel permits into his hand and he left the compartment. I seated myself and sat drumming my fingers with rage and frustration. I could almost have wished that Gregori's attempts to safeguard my privacy might fail, so that I should have the opportunity of meeting this Russian hunter of young women and giving him a piece of my mind. While I sat, I could hear the sounds of disturbance as the search parties moved along the train from each end, nearing the middle where our carriage lay. After a while I could stand the wondering no longer and rose, intending to go and see what was going forward.

'I had reached the door of my compartment when it burst open and Gregori plunged in, shooing me away and back to my seat. He was clutching my papers and tears were streaming down his face. I fell back into my seat and he took a seat opposite me.

'"What is it, Gregori? What is it?" He looked up at me, and his dark eyes were swimming in tears. "They will find her," he said. "They will find her."

'He had hardly spoken the words when I heard a door flung open near the end of our carriage and a burst of shouting. Above it rang the unmistakable cry of a terrified woman. I could stand no more. I sprang up, fully intending to see what was toward, but Gregori leapt up also and thrust me bodily back into my seat. "You must not, Mrs Fordeland. You must not. I beg you, for your own safety, do not try to intervene." "But I am a foreign national – a journalist," I protested. "Surely, they must take note of my presence and my views!"

'He stared at me like a madman. "You must not," he repeated. "You are not in America or in Britain now. You are on the steppes of Russia where the law is what the rich say it is. Believe me, madam, if you intervene they will think nothing of killing you."

'"They would not dare," I said. He shook his head. "There is no dare," he said. "They take no risk. You are a very long way from any embassy or consulate which might intervene on your behalf. If you stand in their way they will destroy you, and when your embassy enquires, they will be given circumstantial details of a tragic accident, accompanied, no doubt, by affidavits of those who tried to save you."

'I stared at him in horror. Despite his pale face and his tears, his words had been spoken in such a matter-of-fact manner that I could not but believe him. Now I was truly frightened. Gregori had made me realize that I was a lone Englishwoman of the nineteenth century caught in a place that might have been the jungles of the Amazon or the Middle Ages. Outside – a few yards away – some tyrant, crazed by wealth and power, was committing some bestiality against another woman and, for the first time in my life, I felt powerless to intervene on the side of right.'

Our guest shook her head slowly from side to side, as though still wondering at the recollection.

'That scream came again,' she said. 'I asked Gregori, "What can we do? There must be something?" He shook his head and his tears flowed again. I stepped to the window and drew aside the curtain. Immediately Gregori sprang up and doused the last of the gas lamps. "Come away from the window," he urged. "They must not see you watching."

'Nothing in Heaven or earth could have pulled me away from that window. I pressed myself against it and peered into the darkness, my vision aided by the total darkness of the carriage. The party of men were still outside, and now they were lighting torches, so that soon I could see clearly that there were about a dozen of them or more. They were big men, dressed in rough, practical clothing and tall boots. Their horses had been formed into a sort of horseshoe shape, its open end towards the train, virtually opposite our carriage, the arena so formed lit by the flaring torches which they held. Then another man joined them.'

She swallowed, as though repressing a reflex of revulsion.

'He was evidently in command. Unlike the rough dress of his men, the newcomer wore a tailored uniform, from highly polished top boots which gleamed in the torchlight to a tailored blue tunic, richly frogged in gold and swagged with bullion piquet cords which swung at his shoulder and sparkled in the light. There was no doubting his rank, his wealth and his authority.

'As he swaggered into the torchlit space, the same agonized shriek split the night, from somewhere close to the train. Two men emerged from the darkness and made their way into the lighted area, dragging someone else between them. When they were illuminated I could see that they were two of the mounted ruffians and that the figure they dragged between them, who twisted and writhed at every step, was that of a slender young woman.

'They paraded her before their uniformed leader like a beast at auction. He stepped around her, apparently saying something, then gestured to one of the mounted men. Something flashed in the torchlight and a knife buried itself in the soil near his feet. He stooped to pick it up and waved a peremptory hand at the two men holding the girl. His henchmen stepped apart, holding the struggling girl at arm's length, so that her feet barely touched the ground. Now their master gestured again and stepped towards one of the mounted men, who handed him something.

'I shall remember to my dying day the scream that the poor girl emitted when the leader of her tormentors uncoiled what was in his hand and she saw that it was a long whip. Two men emerged from the dark and removed her hat, letting her long black hair tumble free, then ripped her upper clothing from her, so that she stood, naked to the waist, her skin pale gold in the torchlight, while the uniformed monster paced about behind her. Suddenly he turned towards her and the whip cracked in the air. As its lash coiled across her naked back she shrieked again.'

Mrs Fordeland stopped and seemed to struggle for self-possession.

'All this, gentlemen,' she went on, 'I watched in mounting horror and revulsion. Every instinct clamoured at me to rush from the train and intervene, but every iota of commonsense told me that Gregori was right, that intervention would, at best, lead me to share the luckless girl's fate. And so I watched this dreadful scene, swearing silently to myself and the tortured girl out there that I would faithfully report the whole episode once I was away from Russian soil. If I had not made that promise, I should never have been able to bear it. As it was, I nearly collapsed as the whip swung and cracked across her shoulders and her screams rang out in the night.'

Her voice dropped.

'But it was not the worst. I do not know how many times the lash fell. I know that I wondered that she was not insensible, that she still twisted and shrieked. Then, with a burst of effort, she pulled free from the hold of one of her captors and pulled away from the other. He stumbled, fell, and lost his grip. Suddenly she was free, and began to stagger towards the train. The uniformed man shouted something and one of the mounted men raised a weapon, sighted and shot her.'

Our client's hands worked furiously at the clasp of her handbag and her head shook at the memory.

'For a moment I stared at the dreadful scene beyond the window – the impassive circle of mounted men, the ring of torches, the strutting peacock in his military finery and the pathetic broken body sprawled in the dirt. That the girl was dead I did not doubt, bringing her the only mercy that they had shown her. Then the horror of it all overwhelmed me and I spun away from the window with a cry.

'Throughout the events I have described, Gregori had sat still, his face covered by his hands. Now he asked, "What has happened?" "They have shot her!" I sobbed. "They have murdered the poor girl!"

'Outside the window I was aware of the group of men riding away into the darkness, their torches trailing away into little spots of light and finally vanishing. Gregori's mouth opened silently at first, then he emitted an awful strangled murmur, as terrible in its muffled way as the cries of the murdered girl, and dropped his face again into his hands.

'When I had composed myself a little, I poured a stiff measure of brandy for myself and thrust a glass into Gregori's hand. He swallowed it at one gulp, then stared at me, his red-rimmed eyes wide. "She was Katya," he said. "She was my little sister."'

Eighteen

Aftermath of Murder

'He stumbled away, out of the compartment, and I continued to sit rigid in my seat. After some little time the train began slowly to move, and I continued to sit motionless, staring out of the window as the empty black landscape passed by. I sat so until the first dawn light began to creep across the plains. Gregori did not return.'

Holmes and I had sat almost motionless as our client told her fearful tale. Now Holmes shifted in his chair and indicated to me that I should ring for more tea. I did so, and the interruption provided a welcome respite from the horror of Mrs Fordeland's tale.

We drank our tea in silence, and I reflected that, in my time with the Army Medical Service and in my civilian practice, as well as in my adventures with Holmes, I had seen a great deal of the cruelty of humankind, but nowhere had I come across an episode such as our client had described.

'Did you,' asked Holmes, 'leave Russia without any repercussions as a result of this episode? It is not, I would have thought, the kind of thing which they would wish to fall under the notice of a foreign journalist.'

'No direct steps were taken against me,' she replied. 'At dawn our train halted at a little town whose complicated name I have forgotten and which was not, in any case, one of our intended stops. Gregori came to me, full of apologies, and pleaded to be released from his obligations to me. His sister's body had been brought aboard the train on the previous night, and he now wished to see her properly buried.

'I could not imagine continuing my journey all the way to

113

Vladivostok without the great assistance of Gregori's presence, and we made an agreement, that I would remain for his sister's funeral, so that we might travel on together. My luggage was removed from the train and Gregori found me lodgings at the only tavern in the little town. He had told me that his sister's body would lie for three days and nights while psalms were read over it, and I stayed there for those days. At one point I visited the home of the Russian Orthodox priest, where Katya's body lay. She showed no sign of the monstrous violence from which she had died, the fatal injury being hidden. She had not been embalmed, merely washed and dressed according to their custom, for anything else would be forbidden by Orthodox practice. In her hands were folded a large white cross and the printed paper that her soul must present to Saint Peter for admission to Paradise, while a strip of paper printed in gold with the pattern of a crown was bound across her brow. She looked like a schoolchild, dressed for a Christmas festival.

'I went to the burial service, still promising this girl whom I had not known that I should make the manner of her death known to the world. Throughout the ceremony I was aware of the presence of a great black-bearded man in a uniform coat and high-crowned cap who stood and watched Gregori. A truncheon with a spiked iron band hung at his broad belt, a symbol of cruelty and violence in these sacred proceedings. Gregori told me that the man was the town's police officer.

'When Katya had been laid to rest, we waited at the station for a train to take us on. Before the train arrived, the same policeman came to the station, escorting what was evidently a more important official. This man took up the stationmaster's office and, shortly afterwards, we were summoned by the policeman to present ourselves and our travelling papers.

'In the little office of the stationmaster, the official who had been with the policeman was seated behind the only desk. He waved us imperiously to two wooden chairs and demanded our travel papers. These he spread on the desk and examined carefully. After a long time he looked up at Gregori. "Gregorieff," he said, "it says here that you are a student of languages, presently travelling with this lady as an interpreter, and that your contract with her obliges you to accompany her all the way to Vladivostok, where she will leave the country. Is that correct?"

'Gregori nodded silently. The official eyed him again, then said, "I understand that a sister of yours was killed in a hunting accident recently. You have my sympathy, and I am glad to see that you are continuing with your duties. That is good. You would be well advised not to permit this tragedy to affect your future. I am sure that you understand what I mean." Gregori nodded again without speaking.

'He turned to me. "Mrs Fordeland," he said. "You are, I see, a correspondent of an American magazine, who wishes to see our country so that you may write about it. It is unfortunate that you were a witness to the death of Gregorieff's sister, but such things happen in all countries and I am sure that you would not wish to exaggerate the event by reporting it abroad. As I told Gregorieff, these things can affect our future if we do not treat them sensibly and allow them to be a part of the forgotten past."

'He took out a cigarette and lit it, blowing the smoke to the side. He stared at me. "I am," he said, "the provincial official charged with investigating this matter for the record. I am satisfied that an unfortunate and unavoidable accident occurred, made doubly unfortunate by the fact that you were forced to witness it. I hope that the remainder of your time in our country is not spoiled by any further accident and that you will be able to tell your American readers nothing but good about us, Mrs Fordeland."

'He stamped our travel papers and thrust them at Gregori, then rose without a further word and strode out of the room, followed by the bearded policeman. We heard their footsteps die away along the wooden platform outside and neither of us said a word until the sound had ended. Then Gregori said, "We have been warned. We have been told the official lie and we have been warned that we must say nothing else."

'We heard the train arriving and went out to board it. The official was nowhere in sight, but the large policeman stood at the end of the platform and watched us board, remaining there until the train pulled away.'

She waved a hand dismissively.

'You will not wish to hear of the remainder of my journey,' she said. 'I had been deeply shocked by the death of Gregori's sister, but I had taken on a task, and it has always been my way to try and carry out as efficaciously as I may the tasks which I take upon myself. Soon we fell back into the pattern which had persisted before, continuing our journey in short or longer sections, usually by train but sometimes by carriage, visiting towns and villages that lay along or close to our route and, in each one, seeking for people and events to write about for my American readers.

'Gregori was just as efficient, though he was much quieter. All the time I wondered how the terrible events which I had witnessed had come about, but I saw no delicate way to broach the matter with him. It was not until we had reached Vladivostok and I was awaiting the vessel on which I would leave Russia, that he spoke at last.

'We had dined one evening and, as we sat at table, Gregori's mind was evidently far away. He ceased to talk and his expression showed me that his mind was completely removed from our idle conversation. I have seen that look far too often in people who carry a heavy burden of grief. I reached across the table and touched his hand. "Gregori," I said. "Nobody can bring your sister back, but I promise you that once I get to America I shall do my best to see that the world comes to know how she was murdered." He stared at me for a moment, then shook his head violently. "No," he said, "you must not! You must not! You will put yourself into terrible danger! You must not do it!"

'I did not understand his outburst, but gradually he began to tell me the story. It seems that his family came from the area where the incident occurred. They and everybody else for miles were ruled by a landowner called Count Skovinski-Rimkoff, a blood relative of the Tzar with an estate about the size of Wales. Gregori had told me, and my journey had shown me, that many Russian nobles are absolute tyrants on their estates, but this count, he said, was worse than any. The count was insane, driven by lust and a delight in cruelty, and behaved, apparently, like the Frenchman Bluebeard. Gregori's family

116

had kept clear of the madman, paid their dues, kept their observances and attracted no attention. Then his parents sent him to Moscow to study. His older sister, Anna, accompanied him to keep house for him – quite a usual arrangement. They left at home their younger sister, Katya, a girl just leaving school, to assist their parents. All went well, Gregori's studies progressed, and then he had a telegram to tell him that his mother was extremely ill. He and Anna hurried home, but they were too late, their mother had died before they arrived. Their old father was prostrated with grief. If all this was not bad enough, the funeral of their mother was hardly over when Katya disappeared. A search was made, but soon the information came that she had been seen being forced by some of the count's henchmen into a sleigh driven by their master. It seemed she had been taken to his home, and it was well known in the area that girls frequently disappeared that way or returned home after a long time in a state of madness.

'The news was the last straw for Gregori's father. An old man, borne down by the death of his wife, the disappearance of his youngest daughter in the hands of a madman was too much for him. He declined and died very shortly. There was nothing left for poor Gregori. He returned to his studies, taking Anna with him again, but he kept in touch with people at home and, eventually, he was able to achieve a secret correspondence with Katya. Painstakingly he created a plan of escape for the girl, found help for her and got funds to her. The final link in his plan was that of accepting the post as my interpreter. By so doing, he could arrange to be on the train by which Katya would make her escape, and he believed that even the mad count might hesitate to interfere with a train carrying a foreign journalist. With this in mind he arranged for Anna to join us on that part of the journey, introducing her as a cook and servant he had taken on.'

She gazed reflectively at her hands for a minute or so. Neither Holmes nor I spoke.

'What went wrong we will never know. Somehow the count detected her escape and realized that she would have made for the train. He intercepted it and I have told you what followed. When Gregori had finished his narrative I was even more profoundly horrified than I had been that night on the train. "This story must be told!" I exclaimed. "The world must know what manner of evil is allowed to flourish in Russia." Gregori shook his head, sadly. "You do not understand," he said. "You cannot tell the story, even in America, for it will endanger all of us, myself, Anna and not least yourself. If you publish the truth, they will know. They have already decided on their official explanation, and they will continue to lie and will say that you have written an untrue story. Because of my association with you, they will arrest me and say that I have deliberately created lies and fed them to an American journalist to damage my country in the eyes of the world. Maybe they will accuse Anna as well. As for you, you will be in America or Canada, but you will never be safe from them. The Tzar's spies are spread all over the world. In every city there are men like that swine at the railway station. They watch people who they consider enemies of Russia and they seek any opportunity to do them harm. You cannot risk it, not for all our sakes!"

'My only justification for not intervening in the torture and murder of Katya Gregorieff had been that I should survive as an independent witness who could carry the truth out of Russia with me, and now Gregori was telling me that I must never tell the story, for his sake, for Anna's and for my own. Unknowingly, too, he had made me fearful in a way he could not suspect. As I have told you, I had created a certain version of my background which had been accepted across the world, and through it I had become a voice and a pen for the oppressed and mistreated of the world. If the Tzar's spies were to reveal my past, then nothing I ever published or said – not just the story of poor Katya – would ever be believed.

'"What must I do?" I asked Gregori. "You must promise me, faithfully, that you will never reveal this story to anyone. I make you the same promise. Go home to America and leave us Russians to do what we must with our own country, but never, ever tell the story of my sister."

'And so,' she said, 'I made him the promise that he asked for.'

Only now, at the end of this long and harrowing tale, did Mrs Fordeland lower her face and weep.

Nineteen

A Warning from Sherlock Holmes

Holmes stood up and went to the gasogene, pouring a large drink for each of us. By the time he had done, our client had recovered her composure and took the glass from him with a steady hand.

'I am deeply sorry,' he said, as he regained his seat, 'to have occasioned you pain by my questions, Mrs Fordeland.'

She shook her head firmly. 'Not at all, Mr Holmes. It is I who should apologize. When I first consulted you I was, perhaps, misled by some desperate hope that this matter could have nothing to do with events in Russia so long ago. Even when you questioned me about my connections with Russia I succeeded in convincing myself that whatever was happening here in England had no possible connection with the warning Gregori Gregorieff gave me in Vladivostok. Perhaps, also, I did not wish to remind myself of my own failure.'

'Your own failure?' I asked, genuinely puzzled.

'If my upbringing lacked in other respects,' she said, 'it served to develop in me a strong sense of justice, most particularly where my own sex are involved. I have tried never to allow my frailties as a woman to prevent me from doing or saying what I consider to be my duty. Where poor Katya Gregorieff was concerned, I failed. I failed at the time because I did not intervene from fear, so I made myself a promise that I would attempt to redeem my cowardice by publishing the story of Count Skovinski-Rimkoff where the world might read it. I failed her in that as well. You may believe me, gentlemen, that there is not a day that passes when I do not remember her. Never do I step on to a lecture platform, never do I take up my pen to write an article, but I remember, and accuse myself for my failure.'

I thought about where this lady had come from and what she had accomplished and I was outraged that she should think herself cowardly.

'My dear lady,' I said, 'I cannot imagine why you should upbraid yourself or regard yourself as having failed in any respect. When I first read your book about your experiences in Mongkuria, I was overwhelmed with admiration for the courage that enabled you to take up the challenge of that largely unknown kingdom thirty years ago. Every word that you have said today has increased my admiration. I have had the privilege of knowing a number of brave men and women, but I do not hesitate to say that you must rank among the first.'

'You are exceedingly kind, Doctor, and it may be that I should have found some way of speaking of these things before, but I had given my promise to Gregori. Had I known that he was out of Russia, I might have felt able to speak earlier.'

'Out of Russia he may be,' said Holmes, 'but someone has set the Russian Embassy's best on his trail. Someone there evidently fears him, as somebody there fears you, Mrs Fordeland.'

'But why should they fear me or Gregori, Mr Holmes?'

'You fear the threat that Professor Gregorieff explained to you – that any exposure of Count Skovinski-Rimkoff may lead to exposure of your own past. That is exactly what the count fears about you, Mrs Fordeland.'

'If I were to reveal to the world what I witnessed that night in Russia and identify the perpetrator, I cannot see that it would be more than an embarrassment to the Tzar in the eyes of the world. The count would surely never be punished for his actions. Why would he fear me?'

'Because there is no effective representative government in Russia, because, in the end, everything rests upon the Tzar's opinions, it is absolutely necessary for anyone who intends to reach the higher echelons of society in that country to take one of two courses – they must ally themselves to the Crown and solicit the Tzar's goodwill or they must take the risk of joining one of the factions who oppose the Tzar and seeking their goodwill. Count Stepan fell into disfavour with the late Tzar, because of an unseemly episode in London when he allowed his bestial habits to run away with him. The result was an incident which brought him to the notice of Scotland Yard and might, indeed, have resulted in a prosecution. I understand that political pressure was applied and the victim of his excesses was paid off. It was not, I imagine, an episode that earned him any credit with the former Tzar. It may be the reason why he has only recently returned to London for the first time since that affair.'

Holmes took his pipe from his coat pocket and began to fill it as he spoke.

'You are a well-informed and intelligent woman, Mrs Fordeland. You cannot but be aware that, since the death of the old Tzar and the accession of Nicholas, factionalism among the nobility of Russia has greatly increased. Even now, so soon after the coronation, there is a group who support the Tzar, a group who support the Tzarina, believing that there is a difference of interest between them, a group who support the Tzar's mother, who, it is rumoured, is against her daughter-in-law, a group who believe that Nicholas is too weak to be a good Tzar and should abdicate in favour of a cousin, and who knows how many other groups.'

He tamped the tobacco into his pipe with his long fingers.

'In such a climate,' he continued, 'the Tzar must seek allies, and such a search will create an opportunity for a man like Count Skovinski-Rimkoff. By becoming a "King's man" as it were, he can expect advancement and preference from the throne, and he seems to have succeeded inasmuch as he is here in London not as a casual visitor but as one of the official Russian party attending Her Majesty's Jubilee.'

Holmes lifted his filled pipe, mutely asking permission, and our guest gave him a nod.

'All of which,' he continued, when the pipe was well alight, 'makes you a very apparent threat to the count. He must know that you live the other side of the Atlantic. He certainly knows that you are a woman famous for speaking her mind on the subject of personal freedom. Why then, he will have asked himself, are you in London now – at a time when his

121

past folly in London has been forgotten and he comes as one of his tzar's representatives? Why else, except to make sure that his past crimes are revealed at this time, when they will become not only a personal humiliation, but also a reproach to his country and a slur upon his royal cousin. I am sure that he fears a fuss in the British press which will result in his recall to Russia and the consequent loss of royal favour.'

Mrs Fordeland stared at my friend. 'But Mr Holmes,' she said, 'you know that this is not true.'

'Certainly,' he agreed, 'but were you or I to assure the count, or Major Kyriloff at their embassy, that your presence in London is entirely connected with your desire to experience the Jubilee festivities and to meet your former pupil, King Chula, they would not believe us. They would assume that these are only excuses to conceal your real purpose.'

'That is preposterous!' the lady exclaimed.

'Entirely,' agreed Holmes, 'but it is an unfortunate habit of personalities much less arrogant than the count's to believe that any incident occurring in their vicinity is related to and aimed at them. Which creates a serious problem for you.'

'I had understood you to say that I was not in any apparent danger, Mr Holmes.'

'So I did, Mrs Fordeland, but that was, with respect, before you revealed to me your connection with Count Skovinski-Rimkoff, let alone the fact that a Russian official warned and threatened you before you left that country.'

'Then you now believe that I am in danger, Mr Holmes?'

'I regret to say that I think you may well be.'

'Then what can I do?'

'The question,' said Holmes, 'is not so much what you can do, but what you are willing to do. You have not suffered the obvious attentions of Russian agents in Canada or America, though I have no doubt that they have kept some kind of watch upon you. If you were to retreat across the Atlantic, I am sure that the danger would vanish. It is only here and now, in London at the time of the Jubilee, that the count perceives you as a threat.'

I was sufficiently astute to catch my friend's use of the word 'retreat'. I had seen him before use words to persuade a client to continue in a course of action that might expose them to danger so that he could conclude his enquiry, and I have to say that I always disapproved. Our client lifted her chin and I guessed, correctly, at her response.

'Mr Holmes,' she said, firmly, 'I came to London with two principal purposes, to enjoy the Jubilee celebrations and to meet King Chula. I intend to carry out my intentions, and with that in mind I shall be grateful for your advice as to how I may do so without unnecessary risk to myself and my granddaughter.'

'If that is your decision,' said my friend, and perhaps I imagined a hint of satisfaction in his tone, 'then I suggest that you stay as close as you may to your hotel, that you avoid lonely places and that you never leave your granddaughter alone.'

'In addition,' he said, rising and stepping towards his desk, 'I recommend that you always keep this handy.' He had been poking about in one of the desk's drawers and now handed her a small silver object.

'A whistle?' she said.

'Precisely,' said Holmes. 'One of the kind carried by every London constable. A sharp blow or two upon it, day or night, will bring every constable within earshot running, and since the capital is more heavily policed this summer than it has ever been, I do not imagine that you will ever be more than yards away from a policeman or two.'

She smiled as she tucked the whistle away.

'What a very ingenious idea! I really cannot thank you enough, Mr Holmes, and I apologize for misleading you at the outset. Now I must settle your fees.'

My friend raised a peremptory hand. 'Watson will tell you that my scale of fees varies only when I decide to remit them entirely. Since your problem has presented me with certain singular aspects which it has been challenging to unravel, Mrs Fordeland, pray let me remit them in your case.'

She thanked us profusely and left.

'Holmes!' I expostulated, as soon as our door had shut behind her. 'It is unworthy of you!'

'Really?' he replied, blandly. 'What is unworthy of me?'

123

'You have successfully unravelled the matter on which she first consulted us and should have warned her, in the strongest terms, to take herself and her granddaughter away from England. Instead you have encouraged them to remain exposed to danger.'

He stared at me thoughtfully. 'You seem to have overlooked certain aspects of the matter,' he said. 'The first is the involvement of Agatha Wortley-Swan, which remains totally unexplained. The second is the perhaps more important question of how to prevent Professor Gregorieff from attempting to murder Count Skovinski-Rimkoff.'

'You believe that is his intention?' I asked, astonished.

'Very definitely,' he said. 'Now, I might inform Scotland Yard and leave it to them, but Kyriloff has already tried to set the Yard on to Gregorieff, without even knowing who he is. I would be loath to take any steps which might put Kyriloff or the count in a position to mistreat the professor, but I do not think that I would be able to persuade Gregorieff away from his intentions. It is a difficult problem, Watson. We have wandered into some very murky waters.'

Twenty

An Unexpected Visitor

'But you said,' I recalled, 'that Professor Gregorieff was not a violent man.'

'So I did, Watson, nor is he. May I remind you that it was you who pointed out to me my error in dealing with Mrs Fordeland?'

'Your error?' I said, for I was genuinely puzzled.

'My serious error,' he confirmed. 'When the lady first consulted us I assessed her as being a person of firmer principle than most, who would not deliberately mislead me. It was you, Watson, who pointed out that a person of impeccable integrity may deem it a part of that integrity to conceal another's secret or to honour a promise given. But for that insight, we might well not have had this afternoon's conversation.'

I was pleased at his recollection of my contribution, but I failed to see the relevance.

'What,' I said, 'has that got to do with the murderous intentions of Professor Gregorieff?'

'It is analogous, Watson. Mrs Fordeland is a person of integrity, which means that she will only deal in untruths or half-truths when there is some principle at stake. Gregori Gregorieff is a man of peace, which means that he will not take to the knife, the pistol or the bomb unless there is some greater reason. He has that greater reason. Two of his family are dead as a result of the loathsome Count Skovinski-Rimkoff's activities, one of them tortured and murdered within yards of the professor while he sat helpless to intervene. That is, I submit, a powerful motive.'

125

I nodded. 'But why did he do nothing in Russia, then?' I asked.

'Precisely because he is neither emotionally nor intellectually violent, Watson. Were he an emotionally violent individual, he would have rushed out into the night when the count's men were holding his sister and let himself be shot down as she was. Were he an intellectually violent man, he would have made some attempt on the count's life in Russia and been executed or ended his days in some Siberian wilderness. Do you not agree, Watson?'

'I follow your reasoning,' I said, 'but having done neither of those things, why should he now decide to kill the count?'

'He will have wished to kill the count from the moment he learned that his sister had fallen into the maniac's hands, but he suppressed that wish, He continued to do so, not least, I suspect, because he has to consider the welfare of his other sister, Anna. So, he leaves Russia and establishes himself in London, where, according to old Goldstein, he attends meetings of the Social Democratic Federation and speaks as a voice of reason for democratic, not revolutionary, change in Russia. Then comes the Jubilee and the count appears in London as an honoured representative of the Tzar. Gregorieff must have seen it as an indication that something must be done to finish the man and he must be the one to do it.'

'I have to say,' I remarked, 'that after what Mrs Fordeland has told us about the count, and what we already know of his earlier behaviour in London, his death would not occasion me any qualms.'

'Oh, I entirely agree with you, Watson. The man is a maniac of a particularly repellent kind and his wealth and position protect him. If it were simply a case of leaving the count to an assassin's hand I would see no problem. But here we have other considerations.'

'I do not see them,' I admitted.

'Firstly,' he said, 'there is the question of Professor Gregorieff. He is not a violent man, but now feels that he must take violent action against the count. Lacking experience, he is likely to be unsuccessful. That will set both Scotland Yard and Major Kyriloff hunting him in earnest. Even if he

126

is successful, the same result will follow. The Yard will seek him, Kyriloff will seek him. If Kyriloff finds him first, he will have Gregorieff tortured to death to learn who his fellow conspirators were, and that threatens the man's sister and his friend Poliakoff if no others. If the Yard succeeds, then Kyriloff will eventually learn Gregorieff's identity. In either case, Kyriloff will discover the old connection between Gregorieff and Mrs Fordeland. Then it will not matter if she is back in Canada. Kyriloff's colleagues will go after her.'

'You mean that Mrs Fordeland is in danger unless we can stop Gregorieff going after the count?'

'Precisely, Watson. Now, perhaps, you see my tactics and my dilemma.'

'Holmes,' I said, and I felt thoroughly abashed. 'I really must apologize. My remarks were unforgivable.'

'Not unforgivable, old friend, merely ill-considered and uttered without a proper analysis of the situation. But they sprang from your desire to protect the fair sex, and that is a feature which I admire in you.'

'Perhaps,' I suggested, 'you could convince Lestrade that Gregorieff was really behind an attempt on the count in Hyde Park. That way the professor will be arrested and—'

'And Kyriloff will learn that Gregorieff was the strangely dressed person who has followed him about and that Mrs Fordeland has a long-standing connection with the professor, dating back to the time of Katya Gregorieff's death and so on. Do I need to go any further, Watson?'

'No, no,' I admitted. 'It was an ill-thought-out idea and wouldn't work. But what are you going to do, Holmes?'

'I wish I knew, old friend. I wish I knew. What is more, there is the question of Miss Wortley-Swan.'

'I confess that I do not understand her connection with the matter at all, Holmes. Are you sure that she is really connected with it?'

'Oh, she is really connected with it, Watson. She covers for Gregorieff, she provides him with employment and a place from which he can carry out his activities around our client. After the Hyde Park episode she stated that she believed he had returned to Russia, yet Gregorieff told us that he "works"

127

for her – not "worked", Watson, but "works". The professor's English is academically correct. He is not likely to have misused a word. He works for her still and she deflects enquiries about him.'

'And you can make nothing of the connection?' I asked.

'I can make many things of the connection, Watson, but they are blind surmises without data to support them. At least one of them fills me with greater foreboding.'

He poured himself another brandy, a sign that he was more than usually puzzled. Since his return from abroad he had not only eschewed his cocaine solution, but had become notably sparing with spirits.

My friend filled his Meerschaum and set about constructing a pile of cushions upon the couch. I recognized the signs and realized that he might sit all night, puffing his pipe continuously, while his great brain turned over and over the pieces of the problem, ordering and reordering them until an answer emerged. There would be no conversation out of him that night, so I took a book, bade Holmes goodnight and retired early.

I lay late the next morning. I could too easily recall the sitting room after one of my friend's night-long sittings, and had no wish to venture down until Mrs Hudson had disturbed him, persuaded or driven him away from his throne of cushions, and opened the windows to release the thick, grey cloud of tobacco smoke that would have filled the room.

When eventually I did rise, it was to find Holmes at the breakfast table, fully dressed, though his pallor and his lack of interest in food confirmed that he had been pondering all night.

I served myself with a hearty breakfast and kept conversation to a polite minimum. Holmes toyed with a slice of toast and stared at the window during much of our meal.

I had finished eating and was taking a cup of tea and a glance at the newspapers when Holmes spoke suddenly.

'I have,' he said, 'but it will not do.'

'Have what?' I asked, completely startled.

'I have reached a reasonable solution to Miss Wortley-Swan's involvement with Professor Gregorieff. Was that not the question you were not asking?'

'Holmes!' I protested. 'No matter how long I have known you it still unnerves me when you appear to read my mind.'

'And no matter how many times I explain it,' he replied, 'you persist in treating it as mind-reading, when it is, in fact, precisely the opposite. I merely deduce the content of the mind from the actions of my subject. It is good practice.'

I cannot say that being thought of as a subject for practice cheered me, but I let that pass in my desire to hear his conclusions.

'Since finishing your meal, to which, incidentally, you failed to add your usual dash of Worcestershire Sauce, you have sugared your tea twice and then left it in the cup, and your perusal of the newspapers has been so desultory that you have ignored the sporting pages. That is, I think, fair evidence that you are distracted by some overriding thought, is it not?'

I laid down the paper and raised both hands.

'I submit,' I said, 'on the condition that you will tell me what conclusions you have reached.'

'I would not call it a conclusion, Watson. I have considered all the possible and reasonable explanations for the lady behaving as she has and for her connection with Gregorieff. One of them, though frightening, makes a certain amount of sense, but I do not have the data to confirm or reject it.'

'Why do you say "frightening"?' I asked.

'Because, Watson, if I am correct, Miss Wortley-Swan is contemplating something which will result in a threat to our client.'

Before I could reply, Mrs Hudson entered.

'I'm sorry if you have not finished your tea, Mr Holmes, but there is a gentleman downstairs asking for you. He says that his business is most urgent, and he brought this.' She handed Holmes a card.

'This is Mycroft's card!' exclaimed Holmes. 'Dated this morning!'

He pulled out his watch and compared it with our notoriously unreliable mantelpiece clock.

'I thought that we must have sat late, Watson, but it seems we are no later than usual. On the other hand, brother Mycroft seems to have stirred his stumps much earlier than is his wont.

This must be important. You'd best show the gentleman up, Mrs Hudson, and let us have some more tea.'

As the door closed, Holmes looked at me. 'What do you think has disturbed Mycroft at this hour?' he asked. I admitted that I had no idea.

Minutes later Mrs Hudson returned with a fresh pot of tea, an extra cup and saucer and our mysterious visitor.

The new arrival was a tall gentleman of military appearance and carriage, though dressed in civilian clothing. He was of middle years and evidently used to command.

'Mr Holmes?' he enquired. 'I am sorry to disturb a man's breakfast, but I have just come from your brother and he felt that I should communicate with you at once. I am Colonel Henry Wilmshaw.'

'Henry Wilmshaw,' repeated Holmes as he shook the man's hand. 'Of course! Henry Wilmshaw! I cannot tell you how delighted I am to see you. Do take the basket chair. You will find it the more comfortable. This is my friend and colleague, Dr Watson. Can I offer you some tea?'

I was completely bewildered.

Twenty-One

A Parisian Occurrence

Sherlock Holmes had evidently sprung from the deepest dismay about the possible outcome of the case to a sudden cheerfulness that usually betokened the recognition of some new data. He settled our visitor in the basket chair and offered him tea, then flung himself back into his own seat.

'I had thought that you were in Egypt,' said Holmes, and then the light dawned on me.

'So I was,' replied the colonel. 'So I was, and expecting to stay there a while, but it appears that Her Majesty is dispensing medals at the Jubilee and my name came up. So I'm ordered back to England to collect the medal and await new orders.'

Holmes nodded. 'And what brought you here, Colonel?'

'Well, I came into town yesterday, parked my baggage and trotted along to the War Office this morning to see what was what. It appeared that another department had been asking about me urgently, and I was sent along to see Mr Mycroft Holmes.'

'And what has he told you, Colonel?'

'Very little, Mr Holmes. Very little. I know he's your brother, but I have to say he made a great mystery of it all, didn't really explain anything, but said I should see you as fast as possible and that the matter was of the gravest importance. So, here I am, Mr Holmes.'

Holmes nodded again. 'You should not blame my brother entirely, Colonel. It is a complicated story and he knows less of it than I do, in addition to which he has the ingrained habit of keeping his cards close to his chest. There is no reason at all why I should not tell you all that I know, but it is a complicated story. At present what matters is that it seems to threaten at least one death and probably an international incident, hence the concern of my diplomatic brother. It may well be that you are the only person who can assist me at present, and I would ask you to do so in the certainty that you will be assisting your country in avoiding an unpleasant incident and maybe saving a number of lives.'

The colonel looked as bewildered as I had been. 'If that's the case, then I shall help you in any way that I can, but I cannot imagine what help you require from me, Mr Holmes.'

'Do you know Agatha Wortley-Swan?' asked Holmes.

'Of course I do,' said Wilmshaw. 'I was very nearly engaged to her years ago, but Johnny Parkes came up on my blind side and took her off.'

'So you knew her and Captain Parkes well,' said Holmes. 'When were you last in touch with her?'

The colonel looked at the ceiling. 'A long time ago,' he said at last. 'Years and years. Of course, you will know how Johnny Parkes died, just as they were going to tie the knot. I was going to be their best man, you know. I was at that wretched party in Paris.'

He paused, and one could see that his eyes were seeing scenes long gone.

'If it had been possible, I would have taken her up, after Johnny was killed, but it couldn't be. I was too much a part of it, Mr Holmes. I would always have been a reminder to her. She shut herself away and I went where the Army sent me. Of course, I heard of her through mutual friends, but all I heard was that she became a recluse for years and then took up some kind of charitable work.'

He sipped his tea, reflectively.

'It was a damned shame, Mr Holmes, the whole thing. Is that what you wish to ask about?'

'Why do you think so, Colonel?'

'Because the job was never done properly at the time. It was all pushed under the carpet because it happened in a foreign capital and there were foreign diplomats involved. So they said poor old Johnny fell in with some French garrotters. I'm sure he did – I saw his body – but there was more to it than that. Still, nobody wanted to know.'

132

'I want to know, Colonel,' said Holmes. 'I want to know everything you can tell me about the death of Captain Parkes.'

The colonel looked at Holmes with a thoughtful expression for a while, then he said, 'I'm extremely glad to hear it, Mr Holmes. Where would you like me to begin?'

'From whatever you think was the beginning, Colonel.'

'Well now, I'd better tell you a bit about me and Johnny Parkes. We were old pals. We'd been at school together, took our papers out together, joined the same regiment. We were subalterns together and we made captain together, and I suppose that's how we both fell for Agatha at the same time. She was a great beauty, you know, pictures in the *Graphic* and that, you could even buy postcards of her, but Johnny and I were her regular escorts. That's both of us, I mean. We used to go around as a threesome. She used to say that it made it obvious that she wasn't going to make her mind up in a hurry and that two escorts keep the mashers at bay better than one.'

He smiled, reminiscently. 'We had some good times,' he recalled. 'Went everywhere together, balls, picnics, riding, boating, always the three of us. Then Johnny and I were sent over to Paris, attached to the embassy there. I was on duty the night before we left, so Johnny took Agatha out to dinner. I remember when he came back. He looked a bit straight-faced and I chaffed him about it, said something like, "Been out with the prettiest girl in London and off to gay Paree in the morning and you've got a face like a boot!" Well, that was when he told me that he'd proposed to Agatha over dinner and she'd accepted him.'

He shook his head slowly. 'I suppose that was all my fault. I hadn't been thinking about marrying, I'd been just getting ahead in the Army and having my fun. Maybe she saw that Johnny was a better bet. I don't know. Anyway, it was done, so one made the best of it, of course. If Agatha was to be anyone's but mine then it had to be Johnny. I couldn't have imagined her tied up with anyone else. So I congratulated him and we had a drink or two and that was alright.'

He sipped his tea. 'So off we went to Paris, and we were going to be there some months, so Johnny and Agatha were going to tie the knot when we came home and I was to be their best

133

man. Johnny and I had some good times in France. Sometimes I had to remind him he was as good as married, but it was nothing serious. He was Agatha's all through. Then she wired him that she and her mother were coming over for a few days to buy her trousseau, which bucked Johnny up no end.'

He smiled again. 'Almost old times it was, the three of us going about Paris, but of course we often had Agatha's mother in tow. That's how we ended up at the ball, really. It was at the Hungarian Embassy and I admit they do put on a good show, but Johnny and I had been sent round all the embassies a couple of times already. You know the game – a couple of fresh young men, might pick up an indiscreet remark from somebody's daughter or wife, that sort of thing. All rubbish really, but that's how these Intelligence fellows think. So we'd done our bit at that game and as to Agatha, well, she'd been going to balls ever since she came out. We wanted to go to a theatre, but you couldn't get Agatha's mother into a French theatre for love nor money, quite convinced it was all too immoral for words. She must go to the Hungarian Ball, so we went along, and I daresay that Johnny didn't mind showing off his lovely fiancée to the world.

'So we put on best bib and tucker and went along. It was the usual sort of thing, lots of uniforms, lots of evening dress, lots of ball gowns, plenty of drink, a huge buffet with lots of foreign food you've never heard of, everybody being dreadfully friendly and chummy with everybody else, even if they'd been threatening war last week. Well, you learn to make the best of 'em, Mr Holmes, all part of the job when you're attached to an embassy, so I had a few drinks and a few dances and a poke at the buffet, and that's where it happened.'

Colonel Wilmshaw looked about him. Holmes saw the look and stepped to the sideboard, offering our guest a brandy. When we all had a drink the old soldier resumed his tale.

'I suppose it was about halfway through the evening. I was in the buffet and Johnny came in, going to fetch something for Agatha, I suppose. He came up alongside me and we were chatting when we both heard this fellow standing near make an astoundingly coarse remark. It would have been wretchedly bad form in any case – that sort of nonsense belongs to the barrack room if it has a place – but it was worse than that. The comment was plainly about Agatha. Now, he said it in French, of course, but the very reason Johnny and I had been attached to the embassy was because we were both dab hands at the lingo.'

The colonel sipped his brandy and shook his head. 'I'd heard the fellow, Johnny had heard him. I thought, "Here's trouble!" but Johnny was ice-cold. He laid down his plate and napkin and stepped up to the fellow who'd said it and tapped him on the shoulder. He swung round and I could see he was a Russian colonel, though young for the rank. He said, "You interrupt me, Captain," in French. Johnny said, "Colonel, you have just passed a damnably filthy observation about the lady who I intend to marry. I require you to withdraw your vile comment and apologize." He said it loudly, in English, and you could hear the whole room go quiet.'

'The Russian smiled at Johnny, and he says – in English too – "Captain, I shall make whatever observations I choose to my friends, without your permission. If they offend you, you know the remedy. You are at liberty to call me out. I shall be pleased to respond."'

'But Captain Parkes could not challenge the Russian,' I said.

'Certainly not,' agreed the colonel, 'and I was about to remind him of that, but I didn't have to. I've never seen Johnny so angry. He was burning with rage and as white as paper, but he had absolute control of himself. He said, "You must know very well, Colonel, that I am not permitted by the laws of this or my own country, or by the regulations of my service, to call you out. Were it not so, I should welcome the opportunity of killing you." The Russian laughed aloud. He said, "It is easy to make bold claims when you also claim the protection of the law, Captain. In Russia if we believe that we have been dishonoured we attempt to kill the man who did it. You, it seems, do not."

'Johnny took a step forward and I grasped his arm. "You, Colonel, are a filthy-mouthed scoundrel and I demand your apology and withdrawal." The Russian laughed again. "And you shall not have it. I have offered you satisfaction of a kind which is, it seems, too strong for you. That is all you shall have. If the British Army chooses not to fight, I shall certainly not surrender." Johnny said, "The British Army exists to kill the enemies of Britain, not to play personal games, but this matter will not end here." "Oh, I think it will," said the Russian, and he walked off with his friends, all laughing.

'I pulled Johnny back, in case he intended to follow. The whole thing had been bad enough as it was. It was going to be the talk of all the embassies in Paris in the morning, and I wanted to make sure that Johnny didn't suffer for it. So far he'd carried himself very well, but you never know how far a fellow can be pushed. I took him out on the balcony and got him a drink and calmed him down before he went back to Agatha. She, of course, had heard some of it from ladies who had been in the buffet, but we made light of it. The Russian seemed to have made himself scarce, and by the end of the evening it all seemed to have been forgotten, except by Johnny. He was taking Agatha and her mother back to their hotel, and I remember that, as he left me, he said, "I'll make that filthy scoundrel smart for that, you see if I don't."'

Colonel Wilmshaw paused and stared into the past he had awakened. 'That was the last thing old Johnny ever said to me, you know. I never saw him again. He didn't come back to our digs that night. Well, I didn't worry much about that. I admit I thought he might have found a way of slipping past Agatha's mother and be enjoying himself at their hotel, but when he didn't show up the next day I got worried. Then I saw Agatha and she said that they'd said goodnight at the hotel and Johnny was going to stroll back to our place. That's when I got bothered and reported him missing. It was five days later that the French police took me to a mortuary to identify his body.'

He paused again. 'I've seen a deal of dead men,' he went on at last. 'Some of them fellows I've messed with and fought alongside. You've been in Afghanistan, Doctor. You know the kind of things that happen to a fellow there. Nothing has ever made me feel as bad as seeing poor Johnny's body, laid out on a table.'

136

'He had been beaten and stabbed, I understand,' said Holmes.

Colonel Wilmshaw nodded. 'There must have been at least three of them,' he said, 'and Johnny had fought like a tiger from the injuries he took.'

'The French police put it down to boulevard assassins, garrotters. Do you agree?'

Wilmshaw snorted. 'Garrotters! Rubbish! I grant you Paris is full of street bandits, but they're not stupid. Why would they take on a young man in uniform, who looked like he could give an account of himself? There are always plenty of old men about late at night to make prey for them.'

'Would he have been armed in any way?' Holmes asked.

Wilmshaw smiled. 'He'd been to a ball, not on manoeuvres, Mr Holmes. You try waltzing with a sword. No, he was in evening kit with decorations. But there was something else, Mr Holmes.'

'What was that?'

'They said it was garrotters, but I remember when I went to the mortuary, the inspector said to me, "We have his watch and his pocketbook. There is very little doubt that it is Captain Parkes, but we require a formal identification." What do you make of that?'

Holmes' eyes blazed. 'They had not robbed him!' he exclaimed. 'They attacked a man on the street at night, beat him, stabbed him to death and did not rob him. Then it was not street thieves.'

'I'm glad to hear you agree, Mr Holmes. I never thought it was, and I tried to make a fuss about the way the French were treating it all. So did Agatha's father, but it never got anywhere. I got told off by the Ambassador for being a nuisance and a hindrance to diplomacy, and then I got shot off to the East.'

'If you did not believe the Paris police, Colonel, what theory had you as to Captain Parkes' death?' asked Holmes.

Wilmshaw looked at my friend without answering for a moment. Then he took a swallow of brandy.

'You may tell me that I'm wrong, Mr Holmes – you wouldn't be the first – but I couldn't help feeling then and I can't help feeling now that it had to do with that damned Russian colonel. I poked about a bit when I realized that the police weren't doing much. It seems the fellow was a member of the Tzar's family. He had a filthy reputation in Paris. Seems he had pots of money and spent it mainly on women, but his habits were so bad that even the French houses wouldn't do business with him. There were some very unsavoury tales about him.'

Holmes nodded. 'Do you, by any chance, recall the Russian officer's name, Colonel?'

'Now, there you've got me. Never was much good at names and he had one of those complicated Russian names.'

'Was it,' said Holmes, 'by any chance, Count Stepan Skovinski-Rimkoff?'

'That's it!' exclaimed the colonel. 'That's the man!'

Twenty-Two

Danger Threatens

'How do you know, Mr Holmes? Is his name in the file?' asked Wilmshaw.

Holmes shook his head. 'Oh no,' he said. 'There is no mention of the count in the official file, nor is there any mention of the incident in the buffet.'

'I told them, Mr Holmes! I told the French police all about it!' Wilmshaw burst out.

'I'm sure you did,' said Holmes, 'but all they recorded was the time at which you saw Captain Parkes leave the ball with his fiancée and her mother and the fact that he failed to come home that night.'

The colonel snorted. 'I knew it!' he exclaimed. 'Because the scoundrel's a Russian nobleman, they covered it up, but you mark my words, Mr Holmes, after his row with Johnny, that man arranged for Johnny to be waylaid and beaten. Whether he intended him to be killed I don't know, but I'm sure he arranged it.'

'I am very largely in agreement with you,' said Holmes, 'but there are two matters to be considered. Firstly, Count Skovinski-Rimkoff is presently in London as an official guest at the Jubilee. I suggest that you are at pains to avoid him. Secondly, and more to the point, the man's presence here poses a danger to Miss Wortley-Swan.'

'To Agatha!' exclaimed the colonel. 'How?'

Holmes raised a hand. 'I am not, at present, at liberty to reveal the reasons for my fears, but believe me, Colonel, they are genuine. Now, would it be in order for you to visit the lady to apprise her of your return from Egypt?'

'Well, of course,' said Wilmshaw. 'I was intending to do so in any case.'

'Then do so this afternoon, Colonel. It is most important. See Miss Wortley-Swan and contrive, if you can, to spend as much time in her company as possible over the next few days. Do not, I enjoin you, tell her that you have seen me or my brother, but stay as close to her as you may.'

The colonel cast a puzzled eye on Holmes. 'Sealed orders, eh? Very well then. If Agatha's in any kind of danger, you can count on me, Mr Holmes.'

When the door closed behind our visitor I chuckled.

'I do not know, Watson, what you find amusing in all this,' said Holmes. 'This affair becomes darker and more dangerous with every passing day.'

'I was merely considering,' I said, 'that you seem to have turned this agency into a matchmaking business.'

Holmes smiled thinly. 'I sent the colonel post-haste to the lady's door in the slender hope that his appearance may distract her from her dangerous purpose.'

'Which is?' I asked.

'Oh, Watson! Colonel Wilmshaw's narrative has only served to confirm what I have suspected for a long time. Whether the count was really responsible for Captain Parkes' death, Miss Wortley-Swan believes so. That explains her curious connection with Professor Gregorieff. Both of them believe that they have suffered grievous wrong at the man's hands and they propose to murder him.'

'Holmes!' I exclaimed. 'You are surely not serious!'

'I was never more so, Watson. The evidence stares us in the face. Captain Parkes was involved in a public exchange of insults with the count on the night he died. Shortly thereafter he is beaten and stabbed, ostensibly by street banditti who are so inept that, having killed their quarry, they fail to take his watch and pocketbook. Colonel Wilmshaw and Miss Wortley-Swan attempt to press an investigation into the matter, but no progress is made and the matter is pushed aside, indubitably for diplomatic reasons. The colonel is sent off abroad, but Miss Wortley-Swan has considerable finances available to her, so she bides her time and lays her plans, part of which is the creation of a charity which concerns itself with Russian émigrés in London, which enables her to seek out a Russian confederate. Perhaps it was her intention to pursue the count in Russia, but now she is presented with an opportunity – he has returned to London. I have no doubt that she is preparing – in the very near future – to avenge the murder of her fiancé.'

I had to agree with his analysis of the situation, but one point puzzled me.

'But how did she come into contact with Professor Gregorieff?' I asked. 'There are so many refugees from the Tzar in London.'

'So there are, Watson, and among their own kind they discuss the wrongs that have been done to them. Gregori Gregorieff speaks at the Workingmen's Club and is, it seems, well known in his community. Old Goldstein knew that the professor had some connection with the count. Miss Wortley-Swan would not have had much difficulty in identifying a possible fellow conspirator, and what more natural than her employment of a skilled interpreter?'

I nodded. 'So what are you going to do to prevent it? You are intending to prevent it, aren't you?'

'If I believed that any plot against the count would succeed, Watson, I might well be tempted to ignore what I know about the matter and let it proceed, but it will not. The killing, or attempted killing, of the Tzar's cousin in Britain will lead Scotland Yard to employ every method to uncover the criminals. They have almost as many spies in the East End as Kyriloff, and it will not take them long to uncover Gregorieff and his lady employer. It must be prevented for their sake, but I confess that I do not know how.'

If I had hoped that the appearance of Colonel Wilmshaw would encourage my friend in his attempts to unravel the matter, I was to be disappointed. Faced with the problem which he had set out, he slumped in an armchair for much of the day, smoking continuously. In the evening he took his violin and began a series of harsh and discordant improvisations which drove me, fairly rapidly, to an early bed.

The following morning was similar to its predecessor, with Holmes breakfasting on toast alone, while answering my pleasantries with monosyllables or not at all. It was plain that he had failed to resolve the conundrum.

Mrs Hudson had cleared our table and we sat sipping tea when we heard some kind of disturbance below. Voices, one of which was our landlady's, were being raised at the foot of our stairs. Mrs Hudson had long learned to maintain an admirably impassive response to both Holmes and the some-times unusual characters who visited him, so that she rarely found it necessary to raise her voice.

'It sounds,' I observed, 'as though Mrs Hudson has run into difficulties.'

Before Holmes could respond, we heard a short cry from Mrs Hudson, followed by heavy feet pounding up the seven-teen stairs which led to our door.

'I hope,' said Holmes, rising and taking a poker from the fireside, 'that no lout has been stupid enough to do harm to our landlady,' and he moved towards the door.

He had barely reached it and was stretching out his hand when the door was flung open from outside, to reveal the enormous figure of Nikolai Poliakoff, dishevelled and breathing heavily. An irate Mrs Hudson rapidly appeared behind him.

'It is alright, Mrs Hudson,' said Holmes. 'This man is known to me.'

Our landlady made an expression of unspoken anger and withdrew. Holmes showed our visitor to the basket chair, which creaked loudly under the Russian's great weight.

'You would do well,' remarked Holmes, 'not to make an enemy of Mrs Hudson.'

'I am sorry, Mr Holmes,' panted the Russian, 'but Gregori told me to bring you this as quickly as possible.' He thrust an envelope into Holmes' hand.

Quickly my friend tore open the envelope and examined the single sheet of paper which it held. As I watched I saw him transformed. The lethargy which had consumed him throughout the previous evening and at our breakfast disap-peared in an instant. His eyes flashed.

'Watson,' he commanded, 'kindly ring for our boots and take your pistol!'

Turning to the large Russian he asked, 'Are you coming with us, Mr Poliakoff?'

'I cannot,' said Poliakoff. 'Gregori said that I was to bring you his message and then meet him at Miss Wortley-Swan's house. I must go,' and he suited action to word and was off.

Once we had dressed, I pocketed my Adams .450 and followed Holmes down the stairs. Although he had a look of grim determination on his face, I could tell that he welcomed the sudden call to action. As he leapt down the steps, two at a time, he called behind to me.

'Come on, Watson! Come on! The game's afoot!'

Twenty-Three

The Bear Snarls

We were fortunate in finding a growler rapidly, and were soon travelling at a spanking pace, though I had, as yet, no inkling of our destination.

'What was the message that Poliakoff brought?' I asked.

Wordlessly Holmes slipped the letter from his pocket and passed it to me. It read:

> Mr Holmes,
> You were visited yesterday by Colonel Wilmshaw. My contact in the embassy tells me that Kyriloff knows this. He is afraid that you and Mrs Fordeland are about to make trouble for the count and he proposes to seize the lady in order to prevent you. I dare do nothing, sir. You must help her.
> G. Gregorieff

'Great Heavens!' I exclaimed. 'Is it possible that he is right? Would this man Kyriloff attempt to kidnap an English lady in the heart of London?'

Holmes looked at me without an expression. 'Watson,' he said, 'you persist in seeing London as the great city which is the heart of the world's greatest Empire, and of course it is, but it is exactly for those reasons that it is the easiest place in the world to commit almost any variety of crime.'

'I'm sure that you are right, Holmes, but to take the lady seems excessive, even for Kyriloff.'

'Kyriloff,' said Holmes, 'knows no excess. If his dreadful masters required it of him, or if he believed that it would serve their purpose, he would not hesitate to kidnap Queen Victoria.

144

Scotland Yard suspects him of a large number of unsolved killings. I suspect him of more. Both of us believe that he is also responsible for a dozen or so disappearances, including that of the Honourable Hermione Anstruther.'

'Great Heavens!' I repeated. 'Then Mrs Fordeland is really in danger!'

'In deadly danger, Watson. Pray that we are in time.'

Suddenly Holmes rapped on the roof of our cab with his stick. 'Cabbie,' he said. 'A whole sovereign for you if you will drop us in front of the hotel, then take the left corner and await us by the gate of the first yard.'

'Done, sir!' acknowledged the driver, and in a moment we were jumping out of our conveyance at the foot of the hotel's steps. Holmes cast a swift glance around, then pointed with his stick.

'You see,' he said, 'those three young men loitering across the way. They are too well dressed for common street loiterers and in the wrong part of town. Those will be three of Kyriloff's bandits, I'll be bound. I hope that their presence means that their master has not made his move as yet.'

He strode up the steps and presented his card to the commissionaire. 'Tell me,' he asked the man, 'have those young men been there long?'

'About a quarter of an hour,' said the man. 'I thought they might be waiting for someone, but they haven't made any enquiry.'

'Has anyone asked after a guest?' enquired Holmes.

'There was a military-looking gent, sir, spoke a bit foreign. He asked after Mrs Fordeland. They told him at the desk as she was in the garden, but he didn't leave no message.'

'I am sure he would not,' said Holmes. 'Let me warn you, that the military gentleman and the young men across the street mean Mrs Fordeland no good. If they attempt to enter the hotel, do not hesitate to whistle for a constable,' and he slipped a coin into the commissionaire's white-gloved hand.

'It seems we are in time,' said Holmes as we entered the lobby. 'Kyriloff will not risk a disturbance in the hotel, but has set his men to watch Mrs Fordeland leave. That is when he will strike. If we are lucky we can forestall him.'

145

A request for our client at the hotel's reception desk confirmed that she and her granddaughter were in the garden. A page showed us the way, and we found them taking tea at a garden table.

'Why, Mr Holmes, Dr Watson,' she said as we approached. 'This is an unexpected pleasure. Do you have news?'

'I fear that it is not a pleasurable errand that brings us here,' said Holmes. 'I do have news, but it is not good. For reasons too complicated to explain at present, Major Kyriloff has formed an impression that you and I are conspiring to expose Count Skovinski-Rimkoff and thereby provoke a diplomatic incident in connection with the Jubilee. His men are watching the hotel's front and the major himself is in the vicinity. I have every belief that he intends to take you and your grand-daughter prisoner.'

The young girl stared at us in astonishment, but her grand-mother set her cup down very firmly.

'That is preposterous!' she said. 'What do you wish us to do, Mr Holmes?'

'It is evident,' said my friend, 'that you cannot remain anywhere in London where Kyriloff's people can find you. If you will be kind enough to make ready, as swiftly as you may, to stay overnight elsewhere, we will leave here and attempt to outwit the major. Once your safety is assured, I can arrange for your luggage to follow you.'

Mrs Fordeland rose. 'Come, Elizabeth,' she commanded. 'We must do as Mr Holmes suggests with all despatch.'

We escorted them to the foot of the main staircase, where they left us to make for their rooms. Holmes detailed me to guard the back entrance to the hotel, and I paced the rear lobby with a hand firmly clasping the pistol in my coat pocket.

It was not many minutes before Holmes joined me, accompanied by Mrs Fordeland and her granddaughter.

'Now,' he said, 'beyond this door is the hotel's mews yard, at the bottom of which our cab should await us. If we can reach the vehicle, we can make our way to Scotland Yard, where I will enlist the support of the official police. It is unlikely that they will act directly against Kyriloff, but they dislike his tricks in London and will welcome an opportunity

146

to frustrate him by any means that they can. After which, we shall find a safe lodging for you and your granddaughter.'

He thrust the door open and stepped out into the yard, followed by the ladies, while I brought up the rear with Mrs Fordeland's bag. We had almost reached the yard's entrance when a figure in a dark coat stepped in front of us, backed by no fewer than five young men similar to those we had seen at the hotel's front. It was Major Kyriloff.

'I am surprised,' he said, taking a long black cigarette from his mouth, 'to see a lady like Mrs Fordeland leaving her hotel by the groom's entrance. I am here to invite you and your pretty granddaughter to pay a visit to my embassy, where there are matters which the ambassador would like to discuss with you.'

'I thank you, Major Kyriloff, but you may tell the ambassador that I must refuse his invitation.'

'But you are a writer and lecturer, Mrs Fordeland. His Excellency is always concerned that the press should receive accurate information about our country. There have been so many calumnies spread in the foreign press that he is at pains to see that there should be no more.'

'Please assure your ambassador that I have no intention of spreading any calumny about Russia, Major Kyriloff.'

'You have heard Mrs Fordeland,' said Holmes. 'Now please stand out of our way, Major.'

The Russian's eyes narrowed. 'Then I must be blunt with both of you. You, Mrs Fordeland, when a guest in our country, were witness to an unfortunate incident which, upon investigation, turned out to be one of those tragic accidents which sometimes occur in the hunting field. That explanation was given to you, in case you had imagined that something else had occurred. I am fully aware that you have not referred to the matter either in print or in your lectures, but now I see you in London associating with a man who is already known to me. You, Mr Holmes, have been at pains in the past to make my work here in London difficult, at the behest, no doubt, of your brother. When, in addition, I know that you have been visited by a certain army officer, it is abundantly clear to me that a plot has been hatched to

147

discredit a member of the Imperial family. It is my duty to prevent such a plot.'

'Major Kyriloff,' said Holmes, 'you appear to suffer from that distortion of the perceptions that drives people to imagine plots where there are none. Watson will confirm that it is called paranoia. Now, kindly stand aside.'

'I have five young men at my disposal, Mr Holmes. I do not think you will get very far if you try the issue with them.'

'I warn you, Kyriloff, I am armed,' said Holmes.

The major smiled again. 'So, Mr Holmes, are my companions and I. Now, might I suggest that you stand back and permit me to escort the ladies to our embassy?'

Holmes had stood with one hand clenched behind him. Now Mrs Fordeland took something from her reticule and pressed it into his hand.

Holmes swung his hand from behind his back and lifted it. I saw each of Kyriloff's bodyguards tense and slip a hand into his coat, then pause as they saw what my friend was holding aloft.

'This,' said Holmes, 'is a whistle of the kind carried by every member of the Metropolitan Police force. I imagine that, at this time of day, there will be three or four constables within earshot, maybe more. Would you care to repeat your threats, or to offer violence to my client or myself under the eyes of police officers? You know as well as I do that there are officers at Scotland Yard who would be delighted at an excuse to lock you up or to have you deported. If you make a move against my client and the rest of our party, I shall give them that opportunity.'

Kyriloff's eyes narrowed and he took a long draw on his cigarette. The pause lengthened, then, without another word, he stepped aside and motioned to his men to do the same. We walked past them in silence, to find our cab waiting on the street.

'Scotland Yard!' Holmes told the cabby. 'I shall double that sovereign if you give us all speed.'

Our driver cracked his whip and we were away. As I fell back in the seat, Holmes said, 'I thank you for recalling the whistle, Mrs Fordeland. It was precisely what was needed.'

'It certainly seemed to do the trick,' she agreed.

'It served for the moment, but Kyriloff will not leave you alone, nor will he be made any the better by being bested. We must still take strong measures for your safety.'

We rounded a corner and, a few yards further on, our cab came to a sudden halt. Holmes leapt up and thrust his head from a window.

'What is the trouble, cabby?'

'The street's blocked, sir. A couple of brewery drays.'

'Go back!' commanded Holmes. 'Go back at once! Go through Little Ayton Street!'

Our vehicle began the cumbersome process of turning in the street and had almost completed the manoeuvre when the cabby exclaimed, 'It's behind us as well, sir! There's a couple more wagons entangled that way.'

Again Holmes sprang to the window and looked. When he turned back his face was solemn.

'He has trapped us,' he said. 'These are not accidents. We have been bottled in by Kyriloff.'

Twenty-Four

A Royal Refuge

'Can you not use the whistle again?' I asked.

'Hardly,' he said. 'I grant you that it will be heard by several constables, but the moment they enter this street from either end they will see an entanglement of vehicles. They will assume that they have been summoned for that reason and will attempt to deal with the confusion. Meanwhile, under cover of the mayhem he has created, Kyriloff and his minions will come for us. I do not like it, Watson.'

Holmes thrust his head from the window again, and I heard him instructing the driver. 'You see that arched gateway, ahead on the left? Take us in there, as fast as you can. Take us right in!'

We started again and soon I saw stone pillars pass the windows as we entered a courtyard of some kind. At last our vehicle stopped at the far end of the yard and we jumped down.

We were standing in a yard, similar to that of Mrs Fordeland's hotel. Holmes beckoned us to follow, paid our cabby and strode into a door at the head of the yard. We found ourselves in a dark corridor which smelled of cooking and floor polish, along which Holmes strode with seeming authority.

At last a green baize door opened at Holmes' hand to reveal a more brightly lit and better-decorated corridor. We followed that until it opened out into a spacious lobby and I realized that we had entered another hotel by its mews entrance.

Holmes stepped immediately to the manager's desk and presented his card. After a few words he beckoned us to follow him up the staircase that curved out of the lobby. On the first landing, we found the corridor entrance guarded by a desk, at which stood a young man of oriental appearance, though dressed in dark formal clothes. Behind him, on either side of the passage, stood two splendidly costumed guards, each richly caparisoned and each with a sword at his side.

Holmes asked our client for her card and presented it with his to the young man at the desk.

'You will be pleased to wait here,' said the young man. 'I shall have to consult His Majesty's secretary.' It was only then that I realized where Holmes' quick wits and his encyclopaedic knowledge of London had brought us.

In minutes the young man reappeared, accompanied by an older man, whose face was creased into a smile.

'Mrs Fordeland, Mr Holmes,' he said, 'this is an unexpected pleasure, but His Majesty will be happy to see you at once.'

At his gesture we followed him between the guards and along a richly decorated corridor to a pair of double doors at the end. These too were guarded by soldiers. The secretary motioned to them to open the doors and soon we followed him into a large room.

I imagine that, in ordinary circumstances, the room served as a secondary ballroom or reception room for the hotel, but it had now been converted to act as the audience chamber of King Chula of Mongkuria. Its walls were hung throughout with splendid tapestries in bright colours, great clusters of palms and bright flowers filled each corner and a sumptuous carpet led from the doors to a low dais on which stood a richly carved and gilded chair.

Seated in this chair was a man of middle years with the handsome and even features of the Mongkurian people, and a small oriental moustache. He stood as we approached and I could see that he wore heavily embroidered slippers, trousers of black silk and a resplendent tunic woven with rich and complex designs. As he rose, Mrs Fordeland and her granddaughter curtsied formally and Holmes and I took their lead and bowed deeply. We were evidently in the presence of the King himself.

'Mrs Fordeland!' he exclaimed. 'Such a pleasure to look

upon you after so many years.' He stepped forward from the dais and took both of our client's hands. 'I had hoped to see you in two days, but you come by surprise and you bring with you the most eminent detective of the world!'

Mrs Fordeland introduced us and His Majesty was kind enough to assure us that he knew my friend's reputation through my published accounts.

'Your Majesty,' said Holmes, 'I apologize for our untimely appearance in your suite, but Mrs Fordeland has found herself in no little danger and, in attempting to avoid that danger, I had no recourse but to throw our party on your mercy.'

'Danger?' said the King, frowning. 'How comes it that a lady like Mrs Fordeland is in danger in this city? But you will tell me, Mr Holmes, while we dine. His Majesty has done his diplomatic business for today and it is time for refreshment.'

He beckoned his secretary and spoke quickly to him, then waved us after him with a peremptory gesture. We followed him to another chamber, where a meal had been laid, and we were shown to places at the table.

Once we were seated and being served, I looked about me. The room was smaller than the audience room, but had larger windows and a balcony overlooking the hotel's garden. Like the principal room, it was profusely decorated with palms and flowers and half of one wall was covered in ornamental bird-cages and I could see that their occupants were not native to Britain. Throughout our meal the birds engaged in a quietly cheery chatter with themselves and with each other.

Of the meal itself I recall little, save that it was excellent and that there was almost no dish offered that I had ever sampled before. His Majesty ate sparingly, as seemed to be his habit, while paying grave attention to Holmes' account of the situation which had brought us to his suite.

When the meal was concluded we withdrew to chairs on the balcony and fruit juices were served. The King was silent for a while, apparently looking over the garden, which seemed to be at its best.

'There is no problem, Mr Holmes,' he said, suddenly. 'Mrs Fordeland has served my country and my family well. It is an honour and a privilege to give her my protection. My entourage occupies two entire floors of this hotel. It will be no difficulty to accommodate all of you for as long as is necessary.'

'That is extremely kind of you, Your Majesty,' said our client, 'but will it not create difficulties for your staff?'

'I am quite sufficient difficulty to my staff, Mrs Fordeland. Everything else is easy by comparison. Please, honour me by accepting my offer,' and he smiled broadly.

'Then I am pleased and honoured to accept your generous hospitality and your protection for myself and for my granddaughter,' said Mrs Fordeland.

'The spirit of my revered father would never have forgiven me if I had done any less,' said the King. 'Much as I know you disputed many issues between you, he had the greatest respect for your intelligence and learning, and much as I know you sometimes angered him, he held great respect for your independence of mind. It was a quality that he valued highly.'

'He was a man of great kindness, as well as a great king,' said our client. 'I have always deemed it a signal honour that he chose me to educate his wives and children and, thereby, allowed me to assist in some little part his ambitions for your country. If I may make so bold as to say so, Your Majesty, you have continued his work as he would have done it, if all I read of Mongkuria is true.'

I will swear that the King blushed. 'I learned as a boy in your class, Mrs Fordeland, that you do not award praise that is unearned, and I value your words most highly for that reason. I have tried to follow my royal father's path and to advance the nation and my people. There is still much to be done and, as in my father's day, there are still far too many people who will offer to do it for us at a price in freedom which we will not pay.'

He reached for a carafe of fruit juice and refilled our glasses to cover his reaction. When he had taken a long draught, he rose and we followed suit. He motioned us to be seated again.

'I must take a rest,' he said. 'My day has been passed, before you came, in listening to engineers from every country in Europe, who want to build me a railway. My secretary will have been making arrangements for your accommodation and

153

he will see that you are shown to your rooms as soon as possible. I am sure that, after this morning's events, you too will wish to rest. I look forward to enjoying your company at dinner.'

He was true to his word and it was not long before we were escorted to rooms on the floor above. Holmes and I were allocated two bedrooms with a small sitting room joining them and, after I had taken a short nap, I joined Holmes there.

'Ah, Watson!' he said. 'I have taken the liberty of sending a message to Mrs Hudson to pack a small bag for each of us. The King's people will collect them soon.'

'Thank you,' I said. 'You know, I have to hand it to you, Holmes. When we were trapped in the street by Kyriloff's thugs, I thought we were really bottled up and in for trouble, but not only did you find a way out, you landed us as guests of the King of Mongkuria. Very well done!'

'I am delighted, Watson, that you have not, on this occasion, attributed the result to luck. The fact is that, as soon as Mrs Fordeland made us aware of her connection with the King of Mongkuria, I made it my business to discover where His Majesty was quartered, in case it became of relevance. What got us out of trouble today was that knowledge combined with my knowledge of London's geography, a basic tool of my practice. It is both foolish and dangerous to attempt a battle, or even to run away from one, unless one has a sound knowledge of the terrain.'

'Oh, quite,' I agreed, 'but you must admit that we have landed rather soft, Holmes.'

'I agree that the accommodation of a royal suite is a far cry from where we might have ended, and His Majesty's generous offer removes the urgent danger to our client, but the second urgent aspect of the case remains beyond my control or intervention and I admit that it worries me.'

'You mean Miss Wortley-Swan?'

'I do, Watson. I am forced, at present, to trust that Colonel Wilmshaw's reappearance in England will distract the lady sufficiently to delay any plans she has for the count.'

Before I could comment, a tap at the door brought a royal servant who presented the King's apologies and asked us to join him in the audience chamber in fifteen minutes.

A quarter of an hour later we made our way to the great room and were shown to chairs alongside the dais. Mrs Fordeland and her granddaughter had been summoned as well, though none of us had an inkling of the reason.

Additional uniformed guards were posted to form a corridor from the main doors to the foot of the dais, and it became evident that a formal visitor was to be received. When all was in place, His Majesty's secretary called for silence and the King swept in. Looking to neither left nor right he mounted the dais and stood before his chair. He had changed into a dazzling white tunic of European cut, heavily braided with gold and displaying a left breast filled with decorations and medals. An expression of stern irritation was stamped upon his previously placid and amiable features. Lifting his head, he snapped his fingers peremptorily.

The main doors opened and a darkly clothed attendant escorted the visitor between the lines of guards. As he approached the dais it became possible to see that it was none other than our old friend Kyriloff, now elaborately clad in the uniform of his rank. He stopped at the foot of the dais and bowed deeply to the King. His Majesty acknowledged the bow with a curt dipping of his head.

'Your Majesty,' began Kyriloff. 'Let me begin by saying that I and the country which I have the honour of representing are deeply grateful for your patience and consideration in agreeing to this audience at such short notice.'

He was evidently intending to go on, but the King cut him short. 'You are here, Major Kyriloff, because I wish to know what it is that you have to say. Please say it.'

Kyriloff bowed again, but it was easy to see that he was not pleased at the King's attitude.

'Of course, Your Majesty,' he said. 'It has always been the practice of my country to extend the hand of friendship to smaller countries and to offer them any assistance within our power. At this time, when the representatives of so many nations are gathered here in London to honour the long reign of our Tzar's great-aunt, Her Imperial Majesty Queen Victoria, it would be particularly unfortunate if there were to be any untoward incident here that spoiled the harmony of the event

155

and caused ill will between the participants, even more so if such an incident were to involve a nation whose monarch has no interest in the matters involved.'

The King's fingers drummed on the arm of his chair and his frown deepened, but he said nothing.

'I regret that I must report to Your Majesty that information has reached my ambassador within the last few hours that a plot is afoot in London, the purpose of which is to sow discord between my country and Britain and to discredit a member of the Tzar's own family. That plot is the work of an American reporter, Mrs Fordeland, acting in conjunction with the British secret agent Sherlock Holmes. I had been informed that both of them had sought Your Majesty's protection when their conspiracy was discovered. I now see that my information was correct.'

King Chula leaned forward and, when he spoke, his voice was low and earnest, but audible across the hall.

'Major Kyriloff,' he said. 'The lady of whom you speak is an old friend of my family and of the people of Mongkuria. For that reason alone it pleases me to offer her my protection. Let me explain to you, Major, what that means. It means that any attempt to inconvenience the lady or to harm her or intervene in her affairs will be seen by me as an interference with myself. Wherever and whenever such interference might occur, I shall make it my business to see that the consequences are visited upon you personally. Now, I suggest that you take my answer back to your ambassador and tell him that you have come close to being flung down the stairs of this hotel by my guards and booted into the street. Good day to you!'

His Majesty snapped his fingers, stood up and swept from the room, while Kyriloff was escorted out. A glimpse of his face showed that he was seething with the blackest rage.

Once the two participants in the little drama were gone, an excited babble of conversation went round among the small number of observers.

'By Jove!' I observed to Holmes. 'That was worth seeing!'

'A pretty piece of drama,' agreed Holmes, 'and evidence of His Majesty's commitment to our client, but if Kyriloff

156

was an enemy before, he is ten times more so now. He has been bested by me earlier and now publicly insulted by King Chula. He will seek revenge. For that reason it is vitally important that Miss Wortley-Swan makes no foolish move.'

Twenty-Five

An Empty House

Dinner at His Majesty's table that night was a fascinating event, though once again the King dined abstemiously and revealed in conversation that, as a young man, he had spent five years in a Buddhist monastery before ascending the throne. Holmes reminisced about his stay in Lhasa some years before as a guest of the Head Lama, and soon those of us present were treated to two powerful minds, one eastern and one western, debating the similarities and differences that appear when the Buddhist belief is compared to the religions of the west, though I have to say that Mrs Fordeland made many a telling point in the discussion.

When at last we retired, Holmes was in a good mood, the opportunity to pit his wits against another superior intelligence having made him positively cheerful. Nevertheless, he warned me that we would have to take steps on the following day to try and stay Miss Wortley-Swan's designs against the count.

At breakfast he broached the problem with the King. We needed to leave the hotel, yet Kyriloff's men would undoubtedly be keeping watch on all possible exits and entrances.

King Chula looked thoughtful and pondered the situation for a short time. Then he smiled.

'Was it not you, Mr Holmes, who commented in the past that the more obvious an event the less real attention will be paid to it?' and he went on to suggest a stratagem that had all of us laughing aloud at its impertinence.

Later in the morning, Holmes and I made our way to the hotel's luggage room, where a range of large boxes stood, gaudily labelled with Mongkurian symbols and heavy stencilling in English which showed that they were to be consigned to His Majesty's palace at Mongkur. A royal clerk explained to us that these contained commercial samples supplied by firms anxious to trade with Mongkuria, as well as personal gifts to His Majesty from other crowned heads. They had been packed ready to be shipped home to Mongkuria.

Soon the crates had been manhandled on to the back of a large carter's dray which was drawn up at the hotel's loading bay. Soon they had been stacked securely aboard the wagon, so as to present the appearance that the vehicle was fully loaded. In reality the boxes had been piled so as to conceal a space at the heart of the pile. Into this area Holmes and I climbed before the rear crates were placed and our hiding place sealed from prying eyes. Moments later we heard the sound of the drayman's whip and felt the horses begin to take the strain as our equipage pulled out of the hotel's yard.

It was a strange experience, riding through the heart of London, completely concealed among the King's boxes, which creaked and shifted about us with every step of the horses, but I would dearly love to have been able to see our progress as an observer. His Majesty's inspired idea had been to provide the dray with a foot escort of eight of his resplendent Mongkurian warriors in their colourful dress, who accompanied the vehicle, four on each side, and from time to time we heard the excited cheers of small boys, their imaginations stirred by our colourful escort. The King was, of course, right. No watcher could have imagined that Holmes and I would leave the hotel in such a very public way.

I rapidly lost all sense of where the cart was taking us, but after a while I caught the unmistakable smell of sea coal and the sound of shunting engines and knew that we must be nearing our destination. The dray made a few more complicated movements then halted. The rear crate was pulled away and the royal clerk stood there.

'We are at Victoria Station,' he said, and looked about him. 'We are in the freight yard and nobody watches us, so you may step down. Once the boxes have been unloaded we shall load up again with empty crates and wait here until you return, Mr Holmes.'

We thanked him and made our way to the passenger ticket office to book to Burriwell.

It was a warm, sunny morning, and the walk from Burriwell Station to the village was a pleasure, but our ring at Miss Wortley-Swan's doorbell was not answered.

Holmes stroked his chin thoughtfully. 'Let us look around,' he said, and we made our way completely around the house. All the doors and windows were closed and, so far as we could see through the windows, there was no sign of any disturbance.

At the kitchen door Holmes paused and stooped, lightly touching the doorstep.

'There was somebody here earlier today,' he announced.

'How on earth can you tell?' I asked.

'The milk,' he said, shortly. 'When the milkcart came this morning a can was filled at this doorstep and a few drops were spilled. They are still slightly moist, so they must derive from this morning's delivery, not last evening's.'

He looked at the kitchen windows, then took a clasp knife from his pocket, slipped its point into one of the window catches and, in an instant, had slipped the lower part of the window upwards.

'Come, Watson,' he invited. 'We have a way in,' and he levered himself into the opening and slithered into the house like nothing so much as a great dark serpent. I was less agile, but succeeded in following him at a second attempt, so that soon we both stood inside the kitchen.

Holmes stood very still at the centre of the red-tiled floor and looked about him slowly. By pointing his stick he drew my attention to certain things, like the two cups and saucers which stood upside down on the draining board, and a folded paper lying on top of a newspaper on the big deal table.

When he had completed his survey he sat at the table and picked up the paper.

'It is a note,' he said when he had scanned it, 'dated today, from Miss Wortley-Swan to her housekeeper. She keeps no resident servants, but the housekeeper and a maid arrive daily.

This note tells them that she will be absent all day and that they may take the day off. It also says that, if she has not returned tomorrow, they should await her instructions.'

'And there is no indication of where she intended to be?' I asked.

'None,' said Holmes, 'and her decision to leave was evidently a sudden one.'

'Why do you say so?' I said.

'Consider the evidence, Watson. It seems entirely probable that Miss Wortley-Swan answered her own door to the milkman and took a can of milk, as though she expected herself and her two servants to require milk during the day. Some time after that she changed her mind and pencilled this note to the house-keeper, who had evidently not arrived by then.'

'Maybe the post brought an urgent summons,' I suggested.

'There are no signs of letters here, but there would not be,' he said. 'Let us look for her writing desk. If I recall correctly it is in the corner of her sitting room.'

He rose and had reached the kitchen's internal door when the front doorbell rang.

'Quickly, Watson!' he hissed. 'Anyone walking round will see us.'

He stepped through the door into a dark passage and pulled me after him, shutting the door behind us. We stood silent while the bell rang twice more. When it ceased I went to move, but Holmes held me back.

'They may do as we did and look around the outside,' he pointed out.

We waited again and, after a while, we heard sounds at the kitchen window.

'You failed to close the window behind you, Watson. Still, there is no harm done. It has served to encourage our visitor to enter.'

He drew his pistol from his pocket and stepped back against the wall of the passage. The noises we could hear indicated that someone was having more difficulty with the kitchen window than I had, but soon we heard boots alighting on the tiled floor. The intruder did not pause in the kitchen, but stepped straight across to the door of the passage.

As he opened the door and stepped into the gloomy passage, Holmes deftly entwined his walking stick in the newcomer's legs and sent him crashing past me to sprawl on the floor.

Before he could gather his wits, I was standing over him with my pistol. Holmes swung the kitchen door wide to let in more light and both of us recognized our prey simultaneously.

'Mr Poliakoff!' exclaimed my friend. 'We seem fated to meet rather unceremoniously. Might I ask what brings you here?'

'Mr Holmes!' said Poliakoff, as he sat up and rubbed an elbow. 'I was looking for Gregori and Anna. Do you know where they are?'

'No,' said Holmes, 'nor, before you enquire, do I know where Miss Wortley-Swan has gone. She left her home early this morning.'

The huge Russian nodded his head. 'She telegraphed to Gregori, at least I think she did. He had a wire and he sent me out and when I came back they were both gone. I did not see the wire, but Miss Wortley-Swan telegraphs Gregori. I think it was from her.'

'I do not like this,' said Holmes. 'If they are up to something rash between them it could all end very badly. We were about to look at the lady's writing desk, Poliakoff. Come with us.'

We made our way to the sitting room, where, as Holmes had remembered, a writing desk stood in the corner. Its lid was unlocked and the writing surface lowered, but nothing lay on it except a blank notepad. Holmes looked quickly into the waste-paper basket below the desk, but found nothing.

'There have been no letters,' he said, and, picking up the notepad, he carried it over to the window.

He had examined the pad for a minute or two when he asked, 'Watson, do you happen to have a cigarette about you?'

I had seen him use the technique before and quickly provided him with a cigarette. After a few puffs he tapped the accumulated ash on to the notepad and spread it out very gently with his fingers.

After a moment he said, 'Ah! You were correct, Mr Poliakoff. The traces revealed by the ash are where her pencil on the sheet above pressed as it wrote her message. It is a

162

telegram to Professor Gregorieff to meet her at Paddington. Unfortunately, the same message has been written twice on two separate sheets and the first one is not so clear that I can distinguish the addressee. Who else has she summoned to join them, I wonder?'

'At least we now know that she is going to Paddington,' I remarked.

'Oh, indeed,' said Holmes. 'A convenient mustering point in London, from which they may have gone to Birmingham, Wales or Land's End, Watson. We have still not found any clue as to why she went or where she is bound, but I fear that the mustering of her supporters indicates her purpose.'

He began to examine the books and documents that were stored in the compartments above the writing surface.

'Aha!' he exclaimed, suddenly. 'Look at this, gentlemen. A scrapbook of newspaper cuttings, all relating to Count Skovinski-Rimkoff. Look!'

We turned the pages and saw that she had filed meticulously every least reference in the press to the count's movements or doings.

'There is no reference to today,' said Holmes as he closed the book. 'It was not, apparently, a newspaper which set her off.'

'It may have been,' I said. 'There was one on the kitchen table.'

'Great Heavens! You're right!' said Holmes, and plunged away through the house, followed by the Russian and me.

In the kitchen he snatched the paper from the table and skimmed through it rapidly.

'Curses!' he snarled. 'Look at this, Watson. She has cut out an item here.' He showed me where a few inches of one column had been cut away.

'It is the sporting page,' he said. 'You read the sports news, Watson, I do not. What sort of item might be in that missing space?'

'It is a sort of miscellany of matters which may interest sportsmen,' I said, 'a sort of gossip column, if you like, about who is preparing what horse for a big race, who has changed his trainer and so on.'

'So it might mention the proposed appearance of the Tzar's cousin at some sporting event?' I nodded. 'What sporting events are there today?'

I went through the paper's sporting pages. 'None that I can see,' I reported.

'Then it is clear what happened here this morning,' Holmes said, in tones of intense frustration. 'Miss Wortley-Swan rose early and took in the milk and the newspapers. In reading her paper she came across an item about the count and promptly decided to act upon the information. She telegraphed the professor and someone else, asking them to gather at Paddington, left a note for her staff that they would not be needed, and set out for London. We know not what it was that she saw in the newspaper, so we cannot follow.'

Twenty-Six

The Missing Piece

We returned to London by the next train. Our last chance was that the little newsagent by Burriwell Station might have a copy of the relevant paper left. But it was too late in the day. The early editions of the evening papers had already arrived.

At Victoria, Poliakoff announced that he was going to Paddington anyway, to see if he could find Miss Wortley-Swan, the professor or Anna.

'I understand your motives, Mr Poliakoff,' said Holmes, 'but I sincerely doubt that you will find any of them at Paddington. If you do, I advise you to be very careful. That they have a plan amongst themselves is plain, but we have no idea how they propose to carry out their intention.'

We shook hands and parted, Holmes and I to the freight warehouse of the station, where our transport awaited us. We were soon concealed among empty crates on the carter's dray and rattling through the streets back to our hotel.

We arrived without incident, Holmes remaining completely silent all the way. Once inside the hotel he asked the staff for copies of that morning's papers and we withdrew to our shared sitting room.

When the newspapers were brought up, Holmes fell upon them eagerly, skimming through them in search of the missing item.

'I have it!' he exclaimed suddenly. 'I was right. The fools have gone in pursuit of the count.'

He showed me the paragraph he had found:

WARWICKSHIRE JUBILEE SALE TODAY

Mr Harry Barnton, the Warwickshire breeder, has decided to take advantage of the numbers of foreign sportsmen who are in England at present for the Jubilee celebrations.

At his Jubilee Sale today he is presenting a fine array of carefully chosen livestock, collected from all over the country and from the continent, in the hope of attracting the best prices.

Among the animals offered is 'Golden Spirit,' winner of the Exeter Gold Cup and the Wolverhampton Trophy. This outstanding horse has attracted a lot of interest and bidding is expected to be keen. Among the illustrious guests expected at the ring are the Duc d'Errennes, Lord Bazelby (the so-called "Backwoods Peer" from Canada) and Count Skovinski-Rimkoff, a cousin of the new Tzar and a bloodstock enthusiast.

'That must be it,' I agreed. 'Miss Wortley-Swan has seen this and set her plan in motion. Can they succeed, Holmes?'

'I doubt it very much,' he said. 'The Russian royal family have been subject to assassination attempts for years, in their own country. How much more careful will they be abroad, Watson? No, they are making a trap for themselves. The odds are that they will not succeed but will be caught in the attempt. Worse – they might strike at the count and fail to get away.'

He shook his head and flung himself into an armchair, where he sat staring fixedly out of the window.

It was a full half an hour before he spoke again.

'Watson,' he said, 'could it be right?'

'I don't know what you mean, Holmes.'

'It is only a few weeks since Moore Agar warned me against overtaxing my brain. You agreed with him. Both of you told me that, if I failed to take some form of relaxation, I should run the risk of losing my mental powers. Do you think that I may have done so, Watson?'

I have seen Sherlock Holmes face the most deadly threats with a sardonic comment, I have seen him apply his great mind to problems that no other intellect has been able to

166

unravel, I have seen him struggle against the most fearful odds and emerge successful, I have seen him wrapped in the blackness of frustration when he could not find a way of solving a mystery, but I had never seen him like this before. Always his outstanding intellect and the methods he has developed of applying it to all manner of problems have been his mainstay. Never before have I known him doubt his own mental processes.

'Holmes!' I exclaimed. 'You are surely not serious?'

'Why not?' he said. 'Why not? Both of you warned me in the direst terms of the risk I ran by continuing to overwork my brain.'

'Yes,' I interrupted, 'and we were right, but you heeded our advice. We went away to Cornwall, you pursued your language researches. You came back a new man. What on earth makes you think differently?'

'This case,' he said. 'This wretched case. It has gone badly astray, Watson, and it is my fault.'

'Hardly,' I said. 'You were consulted by Mrs Fordeland. You have painstakingly unravelled the extraordinary history of the connection between her and the Russian count – despite her attempts to conceal it – and, when our client and we were threatened by Kyriloff's hoodlums, your quick wits found us not only a way out, but a safe stronghold. How on earth can you say that the case has gone badly astray?'

'I am a creature of reason, Watson. I have worked hard to make myself so – to avoid all traces of sentiment or unreason, all indications of emotion when dealing with a problem. Now I find myself filled with foreboding, coupled with a sense of guilt.'

'Nonsense!' I said. 'You have rightly predicted that Agatha Wortley-Swan and her friends have a plan against the count. You, not unnaturally, fear an outcome which will add to the tragedies already suffered by the lady and by Professor Gregorieff. None of this is sentiment or unreason, Holmes. It is merely that the ordinary workings of your extraordinary mind have suggested to you that a calamity is the most likely outcome. I fear you are right, but I see no reason why you should blame yourself. Miss Wortley-Swan, and the professor, chose to keep their plans secret from you. What more could you have done? I fear, Holmes, that we must merely await the outcome and hope for the best.'

He granted me a wan smile. 'Hope for the best! Always your motto, eh, Watson? My good old friend, there have been many times in the past quarter of a century when I valued your sturdy optimism at my side, and many times when I was abroad that I have missed it. You are quite right. We must simply hope for the best.'

Despite my distress at seeing my friend so low in his own esteem, his words touched me. I believe that they may have been the longest compliment that he ever paid me.

'You have done your best, Holmes,' I asserted stoutly. 'Nobody could have done any more.'

I had barely spoken when there was a tap at the door, heralding an hotel employee with a newspaper.

'You asked for the morning papers, Mr Holmes,' he said. 'Perhaps you would like the latest evening edition.'

I tipped him and passed the paper to Holmes, in the hope maybe of distracting him from his mood of self-doubt. He gazed at it with lacklustre eyes and began to turn its pages slowly with no show of interest.

'Great Heavens!' he ejaculated suddenly. 'Watson, where is Mrs Fordeland?'

'I believe that they said she was in the luncheon salon when we came back,' I said, mystified.

'Come!' he commanded, and, rolling the newspaper in his fist, strode out of the room. Delighted to see his sudden recovery of enthusiasm, I followed after him completely mystified.

We found our client and her granddaughter in the luncheon salon, where they were amusing themselves by talking to a Javanese Hill Mynah which had that species' uncanny ability to mimic human voices and was passing remarks in the solemn tones of King Chula.

'I suggest that you be seated, ladies,' said Holmes. 'I have some astonishing news for you.'

They looked at us wonderingly, but followed his suggestion. When they were seated, Holmes unfolded the newspaper

168

and read aloud: '"Fatal Railway Accident at Paddington. Death of a Jubilee Guest. This newspaper was almost ready for press when we had word of a fatal tragedy on the Underground railway station at Paddington. It appears that a passenger who had arrived from Birmingham via the main line was awaiting an Underground train when he missed his footing and fell from the platform, directly in the face of an arriving train, so that he was instantly killed. We are informed that the victim of this tragedy was none other than a foreign visitor to London, indeed, one of Her Majesty's guests at her forthcoming celebration, Count Stepan Skovinski-Rimkoff, a distinguished member of the Imperial Court and a cousin of the new Tzar. Inspector Lestrade of Scotland Yard, one of the officers whose especial duty it is to protect Her Majesty's guests, was summoned to the scene at once. He assures us that the matter was an unforeseeable tragedy, brought about by the crowding of the platform and the large numbers of persons visiting the capital at present."'

There was a silence after my friend had read the astonishing news, then Mrs Fordeland said, 'I do not think that I would have wished him dead, for all his evil cruelty. Does this mean that it is all over, Mr Holmes?'

'I am sure of it,' said Holmes.

'But Holmes,' I objected, 'surely this will make Kyriloff worse! He will believe that the plot he talked about really existed. Will he not come after Mrs Fordeland again?'

'He might wish to,' agreed Holmes, 'but he is unlikely to have the opportunity. The Tzar's cousin has been killed in London while under the especial protection of Major Kyriloff. I imagine that the major will soon be summoned to Russia to explain himself, and a pretty poor explanation he has – that he was besieging the King of Mongkuria's entourage in a hotel because he believed in a non-existent plot to kill the count, while the count was meeting his death elsewhere.'

As so often, events followed Sherlock Holmes' prediction. By next morning there was no sign of Kyriloff's roughs about the hotel and Holmes and I were soon able to take our farewells of our client and the King of Mongkuria and return to our accustomed haunts.

We had not been long returned to Baker Street when Lestrade paid us a call.

'You remember,' he said, once comfortably ensconced in the basket chair with a brandy and a cheroot, 'that silly business in Rotten Row, Mr Holmes?'

'Of course I do,' said Holmes.

'It was good of you to help us out there. We might have wasted a deal of time and effort chasing about after imaginary assassins.'

'I'm sure you would have seen through Major Kyriloff's ruse eventually,' said Holmes, without a trace of a smile.

'I had a nasty moment a couple of days ago, though. I was told that the very same man – that same Russian count – had been killed at Paddington tube station. I had a few unpleasant thoughts, I can tell you. Suppose it had been all proper at Rotten Row and somebody really was trying to nobble him? There'd have been hell to pay and heads to roll at the Yard, I can tell you!'

'It was an accident, was it not?' asked Holmes.

'So it was, Mr Holmes, and I was never more relieved in my life. I was down there like a whippet, but there was no doubt about it. He was standing in the crowd on the platform and, just as a train came in, he turned about and lost his balance, went straight in front of the train.'

'You were able to establish this?' said my friend.

'Oh, indeed, Mr Holmes. Of course, not many people noticed till it was over. There was a foreign couple right beside him, but they didn't speak much English, and there was an English lady, but she was hysterical, poor lady. It happened right in front of her and she could barely speak about it. Luckily there was one witness who saw all that happened. There was a soldier there, a Colonel Wilmshaw. He was very useful, gave us a complete account, like a military report.'

'And you are sure it was an accident?' persisted Holmes.

'Oh, definitely. What else might it be?'

'It occurred to me,' said Holmes, 'that, after the spurious incident in Rotten Row, Major Kyriloff might be trying to create the impression that the count was in danger so that he could dispose of him in due course.'

'I thought of exactly that, Mr Holmes, as soon as I heard. Luckily Colonel Wilmshaw rules that out, but I did check up where Kyriloff was at the time. It seems that he has an interest in the King of Mongkuria and was hanging about the King's hotel.'

'Perhaps,' suggested Holmes, 'the Tzar intends to invade India by way of Mongkuria, though it would be the long way round.'

'Perhaps,' agreed the little policeman. 'But there's another aspect of the thing that really intrigues me, Mr Holmes. Do you believe in fate?'

'I believe that a certain course of action, if persisted in, will lead inevitably to a certain result, if that's what you mean, Inspector.'

Lestrade shook his head. 'No, no. I mean that Kyriloff set up his silly joke in Hyde Park as though the count was to be killed and, blow me, days later the count dies by accident! I know you don't believe in coincidence, Mr Holmes, but isn't that a bit curious?'

'You are becoming metaphysical, Lestrade,' said Holmes. 'It is not good for a scientist. It will mislead you. Stick to what is proven and to what is reasonable inference from what is proven. People who deal in the unprovable are not scientists – they are mystics. A detective must be a scientist.'

When Lestrade had left us, Holmes shut the door behind us with a thoughtful expression.

'Wilmshaw!' he said, quietly. 'I should have realized that the second telegram went to him. So far from distracting Miss Wortley-Swan from her purpose, I innocently sent her the means. A combination of a peace-loving academic and a lady driven by two decades of grief would be unlikely to achieve a successful assassination, but I added an able professional soldier.'

'You intend to let matters lie, then?' I asked.

'What would you do, Watson? You have the advantage of me. You have been married. At an early age I perceived the effect that women exercised upon me and steeled myself to avoid that response so that I might pursue my rational side. Still, I believe that the death of Skovinski-Rimkoff is not one that requires vengeance. If I were called to my account tonight, Watson, I would like to believe that I have left the world a little better. The law of three countries has failed to punish the count. I see no difficulty in leaving him to the justice of Miss Wortley-Swan.'

Although he often referred afterwards to the case as one of his failures, the knowledge that it was he who had involved Colonel Wilmshaw in the affair seemed to lift the dark blight that had struck Sherlock Holmes when he thought that the conspirators would fail.

Her Majesty's Diamond Jubilee proceeded, unhindered by the death of the count, and Colonel Wilmshaw duly received the decoration which had brought him to London. It was some weeks later that Holmes drew a newspaper announcement to my attention.

'You remarked on one occasion,' he said, 'that I was in danger of converting this agency into a matrimonial service. It seems that my first adventure in that direction has been a good deal more successful than my poor efforts at detection.'

It was an announcement of the forthcoming marriage of Miss Agatha Wortley-Swan and Colonel Wilmshaw.

Author's Notes

With *Sherlock Holmes and the King's Governess* I have done as I have with the previous manuscripts which I have edited, and attempted to find within the text internal proof that this story is indeed by John H.Watson.

This is not easy. I have written in my notes to other manuscripts about the difficulties of having no positively verifiable specimen of Watson's handwriting, the problems of his carelessness about chronology and the strange mixture of real and invented names for places and people which he used.

When Stephen Kendrick's *Night Watch: A Long Lost Adventure in which Sherlock Holmes meets Father Brown* appeared in 2001 (Berkley Prime Crime, New York) there was brief hope that new and verifiable Watson material had surfaced, inasmuch as Kendrick claimed that the manuscript he presented had been supplied to him by Watson's daughter(!) accompanied by a codicil to the Doctor's will.

Alas, the manuscript does not live up to expectations. On the first page of his introduction, Kendrick misstates the date of Sir Arthur Conan Doyle's death by three years, leaving the reader cautious as to what may follow. What follows is, indeed, a fascinating story, but cannot be from Watson's pen. The manuscript is clearly of American origin. Watson would never have written a three-word 'sentence' containing no verb, nor would Holmes have spoken of someone as being 'slightly aghast', which reminds one of bad jokes about being 'slightly pregnant'. Holmes cannot have employed 'momentarily' in the American sense. In America it means 'in a moment; in Britain it means 'for a moment'. Watson is casually addressed as 'Mr' by persons who know him to be a doctor and Holmes' age is misstated (one of the few facts about Holmes' life that we know from the canon is that he was born in 1854). Not only would Watson not have used the American 'stoop' for a doorstep, he would probably not have known what it meant. Finally, though I hesitate to claim one of the manuscripts which I have edited in evidence, if *Sherlock Holmes and the Rule of Nine* (Severn House, 2003) is authentic, then Holmes and Father Brown had their first meeting in 1895, not 1902.

So, regretfully, the promise of an authentic Watson document fades and, as before, I am forced to research aspects of the narrative in the hope that they will provide proof. The extent to which I have succeeded, like the authenticity of the text, is a matter for individual readers. To assist them in reaching their own conclusions, I append below my notes on some of the avenues which I have pursued.

One

While confusion usually revolves around Watson's dates and personal names, we appear to be lucky here. There seems no doubt that 'Mrs Fordeland' is, in fact, Mrs Anna Leonowens, heroine of *Anna and the King of Siam*, *The King and I* and *Anna and the King*.

The client's identity serves also to confirm Watson's date. Mrs Leonowens left Siam in 1868, to visit her daughter who had been left in an English boarding school. During the lady's absence from Siam, the King died and was succeeded by his eldest son, Anna's former pupil. As he was then only fifteen, a regency ruled the country and did not invite the lady to return. From England she moved on to the United States and later, when her daughter married a Canadian banker, established herself with her daughter's family in Nova Scotia. In 1897, when she had been largely forgotten in Britain, she returned for a visit to the Diamond Jubilee and also to meet with her former pupil, the King of Siam, who was in London for the ceremony.

If this story is Watson's work, one must have a certain sympathy with him in his efforts to conceal and fictionalize the identity of a client who, unknown to him, was going to be world-famous by the time his account was published.

Two

In the latter years of the nineteenth century, the Tzar's Russia maintained an elaborate network of spies and informers in Britain, many of them based in London's East End. There is a persistent rumour that the young Joseph Stalin was an informer for this network, cheerfully using it to destroy political opponents.

The reason for the spying was that revolutionary Russians would leave Russia and settle in Western European countries, where they could continue their plots against the Tzar's regime. One by one the Tzar persuaded European governments to make life unpleasant for these plotters, so they tended to move on to England, where a more liberal regime left them alone as long as they caused no mischief in Britain.

Three

Throughout Watson's accounts of Holmes' enquiries there are descriptions of the detective's extraordinary ability at disguise and the numbers of times when he fooled his old friend, even at close range. I had always believed that Watson was exaggerating Holmes' skills, until I discovered that the American film star Danny Kaye (David Kaminski) had similar abilities. It seems that, when shooting was delayed by a technical problem one day, Kaye had the studio make-up artists turn him into an old man and took a taxi to his home. Having told the studio switchboard that all calls from his family were to be met with the statement that Mr Kaye was on the set and could not be disturbed, he presented himself to his own family as an elderly distant relative who had arrived from Russia speaking no word of English. Apparently he drove them crazy for hours before he admitted the imposture. So, maybe Sherlock Holmes was as good as Watson would have us believe.

In *A Study in Scarlet*, the first of Watson's published

175

accounts of Holmes' cases, he tells us that, after taking his medical degree, he took the course for intending army surgeons at the Royal Military Hospital at Netley in Hampshire. There is a long note on this great and strange building in my *Sherlock Holmes and the Harvest of Death*. Among the facilities it offered was an in-house postcard-printing shop to supply the sick and their visitors with souvenirs. Sadly, only the hospital's chapel now survives.

Four

Mycroft's use of the term 'gay' is not meant to imply that the girl was a Lesbian. From at least the eighteenth century until comparatively recently the word was used to mean 'randy, promiscuous or immoral'. As a verb it could mean 'to copulate' and 'gaying stick,' 'gaying pole' or 'gaying pintle' referred to the male member. The standard prostitute's come-on query was 'Are you gay?' It was the survival of that expression among American homosexuals, meaning 'Are you looking for action?' that brought about the modern use of the term to mean 'homosexual', rather than the alleged derivation from 'Good As You!'

The misbehaviour of royal and diplomatic visitors is always a problem to the host government, no less so today than in the 1890s. As to Russian noblemen misbehaving abroad, one has only to consider that the Russian Crown Prince himself, Nicholas who became the last Tzar, was involved in an incident in Japan in 1891. Nicholas and other assorted royalty were, it seems, sampling the delights of Otsu when, perhaps at the instigation of the homosexual Prince George of Greece, they visited a male brothel. Prince George mistreated a Japanese youth and the party fled. A Japanese police officer stopped Nicholas, who was returning from a temple by rickshaw, and laid about the future Tzar with his sword, inflicting a severe blow on Nicholas' head and having to be stopped and tied up by the rickshaw drivers. The whole incident was a grave embarrassment to Japan, though they got their revenge when Nicholas became Tzar by defeating his army and his navy and forcing him to evacuate Manchuria. The injury to the head caused Nicholas headaches for the rest of his life. Who knows what effect it may have had on the future of Russia?

Seven

Watson's comments on the Khodynka Meadow incident refer to an event which happened three days after the coronation of Nicholas and Alexandra. A public festival for the people of Moscow had been set up by the Tzar's uncle, the mayor of Moscow. Gifts of sweetmeats, a printed handkerchief and a commemorative tumbler were to be distributed. By early in the day more than 400,000 people had mustered. Rumours spread that there would not be enough gifts to go round. The crowd became restless, barriers collapsed and thousands were crushed in the panic that followed. Russians never forgot the incident, continuing to blame the Tzar's German wife. The enamel cup distributed on that dreadful day became known as the 'Cup of Tears' and is much sought after by collectors of Royal Commemoratives. The writer recalls seeing one displayed at Bilston Art Gallery in a Jubilee exhibition in 1977. It is a white enamel tumbler, printed with a coat of arms in red, blue and gold, with the cipher of Nicholas and Alexandra and a motto in Russian.

Eight

A 'growler' was a four-wheeled, horse-drawn, cab, as opposed to the lighter, two-wheeled, hansom cab. The growler took its familiar name, I believe, from the characteristic sound of its heavier wheels on the street.

Nine

Watson's description of Rotten Row in the late nineteenth century is admirably discreet. It was, as he says, the place to 'see and be seen' and was also a wonderful place for meeting new people in society or making covert assignations with sexual partners. While the horse riders might include actresses,

177

royalty, soldiers, politicians, sportsmen and almost anyone from the upper middle class upwards, there is no doubt that many of the beautiful and expensively dressed women who rode in the Row were making a very good living there.

Ten

Watson's initial meeting with Holmes is described in *A Study in Scarlet*, the first of Watson's published records of a Sherlock Holmes enquiry. Watson, a military doctor, had been injured in Afghanistan and subsequently contracted fever. His health damaged, he was returned to England and placed on half pay. He had no family in Britain and soon found himself at a loose end in London, overspending on his half pay in search of company. It was early in 1881 that a friend introduced Watson to Holmes, who was working at the London Hospital, carrying out a series of experiments in post-mortem bruising by beating the cadavers in the dissecting room. Holmes had discovered a set of rooms to rent and required a flatmate. The deal was done and the immortal partnership forged.

Eleven

The three brass balls which hang by tradition outside pawn-brokers' shops are actually a symbol of three bags of gold in honour of Saint Nicholas.

The saint whom we know better as Santa Claus, Sinter Klaas or Father Christmas, is the patron saint of children, sailors, thieves and pawnbrokers.

Nicholas, who was a bishop of the early Christian Church at Myra in Asia Minor, was orphaned in his childhood but inherited great wealth. Nevertheless, he grew up to be a kindly and concerned young man. A legend tells that Nicholas heard of a poor man with three daughters, bewailing the fact that he had no money to provide his daughters with a dowry. Nicholas sneaked into the man's house (by the chimney – how else?) and left a bag of gold. So the first daughter was married and Nicholas repeated the trick. After the second girl was married, their father guessed that there might well be a third

gift, so he kept watch at night to thank his unknown bene-
factor. So it was that Nicholas' kindness was revealed and
three bags of gold became the symbol for him as a saint.

The golem is a monster of Jewish legend, supposedly a
large crudely humanoid thing made from clay. The story is
usually told about the Great Rabbi Loew of Prague, who
became deeply concerned by the hard lives led by his people.
Seeking ways to alleviate their hardship he came across an
ancient document which described how to make a humanoid
creature from the clay of the River Moldavka. The Rabbi made
such a creature and recited the chant, 'Shanti, Shanti, Dahat,
Dahat!' whereupon the creature came to life and would obey
the Rabbi's instructions. Soon the Rabbi realized that the golem
would be more useful if he didn't have to tell it everything,
so he taught it to read so that it could learn what it needed to
know. Armed with its great strength and newly acquired knowledge, the golem became a kind of Frankenstein's monster. An
American urban legend says that the golem has now mastered
the Internet and that American youngsters receive emails from
the golem, luring them into dangerous situations.

Twelve

I am reminded by the text that we have never, so far as I
know, learned what became of Sherlock Holmes' Stradivarius
violin. It cannot, surely, be one of the ones that hang in various
Holmesian museums and displays? Without the connection to
the Great Detective the instrument would be hugely valuable.
What price would it fetch if the association could be proved?
Has it been carelessly destroyed or equally carelessly disposed
of, so that somebody somewhere is playing what may be the
world's most valuable violin?

The Irregulars were, of course, the so-called Baker Street
Irregulars, a team of street ragamuffins employed by Sherlock
Holmes to act as his eyes and ears all over London, to go
where he could not go and to carry out errands for him.

Sherlock Holmes, according to Watson, was skilled in a
Japanese martial art which Watson calls 'baritsu', and here
Holmes confirms that his instructor was Japanese. While we

tend to think of eastern wrestling as characteristically Japanese, in fact it is believed that many of the techniques involved originated on the Indian continent and passed, via China, to Japan. Over the centuries many different forms and specialities have developed, and it is not impossible that there is (or was) a fighting art called 'baritsu', but no one seems to have tracked down any reference to it. The name may, of course, derive from a mishearing by Watson, by his own inability to read his notes or from a printer's inability to read Watson's medical handwriting!

Thirteen

Holmes, as we know, was missing from England (and largely from Europe) from the spring of 1891 for three years, the so-called 'Great Hiatus'. Whether or not it was the disappearance and reported death of Holmes which brought it about, there was an upsurge in acts of violence by alleged anarchists in that period, both on the Continent and in Britain. In France it culminated in the arrest of the murderer Ravachol, a savage multiple killer who had terrified France. We, sadly, are more familiar with the kind of pervert who wraps his bloodlust in politics, piety or both.

In England the situation culminated with the only successful prosecution of alleged anarchist terrorists at Stafford Assizes in April 1892. Ravachol's dramatic arrest in France was reported in the British press during their trial, which must have helped their chances no end!

The ringleader, to whom Holmes and Watson refer, was a man named Deakin, a booking clerk from Walsall and organizer of a 'Socialist Club', which operated in a rented house immediately alongside the town's police station. His co-accused were workingmen and tradesmen who belonged to the club, and the accusation was that they had used the club as a front for the manufacturing of bombs to be used in Russia.

In December 1891 Walsall's police chief informed Scotland Yard that he was suspicious of the club's activities. Secret Department officers (including the redoubtable Inspector Melville, later to become one of MI5's first spies) were sent to the town, observation was kept on the club and its officers and, early the following year, arrests were made. The arrested men were kept in what was known as the 'Black Hole' under Walsall's Guildhall, so called for the not unreasonable cause that it was a set of cells deep underground and painted black throughout. After weeks in such custody, fed only on bread and water, Deakin was taken from his cell in the small hours and fed whisky, after which he signed a lengthy 'confession'. When the case came to Stafford, the men were not, by the law of the day, permitted to give evidence in their own defence. Self-appointed, unqualified, 'experts' in explosives gave evidence, and a handwriting 'expert' whose expertise had been comprehensively trashed in the Parnell Commission Enquiry, costing *The Times* a third of a million for relying on his wrong opinion. The Judge knew how Deakin's 'confession' had been obtained, but deemed it good evidence and Deakin and three others were convicted. Two were acquitted. Those convicted got ten years, apart from Joe Deakin, who got five (presumably because of his susceptibility to alcohol!). He was released in December 1897 and returned to Walsall, where he lived above his sisters' drapery shop and kept their books. In time he became secretary of Walsall Trades Council. He is remembered by a blue plaque over the shop front of the building at the southern end of Stafford Street where his sisters kept their shop. He lived well into the twentieth century and I have met people who knew him.

It was believed among anarchists and socialists in the 1890s that Deakin and his comrades were the victims of an agent provocateur called Coulon, an alleged professor of languages. It may well have been true. The Autonomie Club was the principal anarchist meeting place in London at the time. See John Quail's *The Slow-Burning Fuse* and my own *On the Trail of the Walsall Anarchists*, Walsall Library, 1992.

Fourteen

If there could be any doubt that Holmes' client was Mrs Anna Leonowens, this part of the manuscript destroys it. The story she tells Holmes and Watson, of her upbringing and marriage,

181

though not the biography which she invented for herself (and which still appears in modern American editions of *The English Governess at the Siamese Court*) accords almost exactly with the account of Anna's life given in Cecilia Holland's *The Story of Anna and the King*, Harper Collins 1999. Nevertheless, mysteries remain. Some commentators on Anna's life say that, while she was born in India, she was sent to a school in England kept by a relative at the age of six, only returning to India at fifteen. Nothing seems to be known of the missionary with whom she travelled, apart from the fact that she lived in his house in India. We do not know whether he was married.

A further mystery revolves around her financial crisis after her husband's death. Thomas Leon Owens (he welded the two names together, presumably when he acquired his commission) had no private funds, according to Anna. Nevertheless, when he died suddenly, she should have had a reasonable pension and the value of his commission (which he would have bought and which would have cost no small sum). Yet she took to teaching to keep herself and children. One would have thought that she might have kept herself and her family in reasonable comfort on her husband's pension.

Sixteen, Seventeen, Eighteen

As I have noted above, while modern researches have revealed far more about Anna Leonowens than she ever did herself, there are still some areas of mystery left. If the present manuscript is authentic, then one of the largest must be the question of events in Russia. It is definitely true that she was commissioned by an American magazine to travel the length of Russia and write articles for them. Her articles were a great success and she was, as stated in the text, offered an editorship by the publishers, but rejected it. Since her articles had been so successful, and since she had published two books arising from her experiences in Siam, it might be thought that she would produce a book on her Russian journey, but she never did so, despite being probably the first western woman to cross Russia. What is certain is that she never left any hint of the events described in Chapter Seventeen.

The reference to 'Bluebeard' in Chapter Eighteen refers to Gilles de Rais, Marshal of France and mass murderer. De Rais (1406–1440) was a French nobleman of enormous wealth, whose prowess on the battlefields of the Hundred Years' War made him Marshal of France (head of her army) in his twenties. With the appearance of the visionary Joan of Arc, de Rais became her most solid supporter, riding and fighting at her side. He was not part of the treacherous conspiracy of French noblemen who sold Joan to the English to be burned as a witch. On the day of her execution, de Rais was fighting desperately to break through the English line and rescue her.

With the death of Joan and the triumph of his political enemies, de Rais retired to his castles. There he frittered away his great wealth in alchemical experiments. He also embarked upon a career of perversion and murder, kidnapping children from nearby villages, torturing, raping, sodomizing and murdering them. His political enemies and creditors eventually secured his castles, notably Machecoul in Brittany, where the evidence of his crimes came to light and he was eventually tried by an ecclesiastical court and condemned to die. Nobody has ever been able to determine with any accuracy how many children died at his hands.

He is believed by some people to be the origin of the European and British folktales about a mass murderer called Bluebeard.

Nineteen

The gasogene was a device (French in origin, I believe) which supplied fizzy mixtures for spiritous drinks, an early forerunner of the soda syphon. We know from Watson's authenticated writings that there was one in the sitting room at Baker Street.

Twenty-One

Captain Parkes was quite right in stating that the British Army forbade duelling. In addition, it was a criminal offence. A colonel had been killed in a duel in 1843 and the Army declared that duelling, proposing a duel, taking part or assisting, or even failing to prevent a duel, were serious offences. Under civilian law, duelling was, of course, a crime, and participants and seconds could be charged with murder if either party died. Neither the military regulations nor the civil law prevented army officers from working off their ill will in duels. In 1846, what was, I believe, the last criminal prosecution for murder in a duel arose. Lieutenant Hawkey of the Marine Corps took offence at the attentions paid to Mrs Hawkey by Captain Seton of the 11th Dragoons. Seton refused the initial challenge from Hawkey, but accepted after Hawkey kicked him in the back-side in public. They fought near Gosport, Seton missing on the first shot and Hawkey's pistol missing fire. The seconds could have suggested that honour was satisfied, but did not do so. After a reload, Seton missed again and Hawkey shot him through the belly. As Seton lay dying, Hawkey and Pym (his second) fled to France. Seton died and a coroner's jury returned a verdict of wilful murder. Pym surrendered and was tried as an accessory at Winchester Assizes, where the jury took three minutes to acquit him. Hawkey, apparently encour-aged by this, surrendered himself and was tried at the next Winchester Assizes where the jury acquitted him immediately. A cheering crowd applauded the judge as he left the court.

This unclear example did not discourage officers (and others) from duelling. In 1878 the Prince of Wales, later Edward VII, challenged Lord Randolph Churchill to a duel. Lord Randolph replied in an insulting letter that such a duel was impossible, whereupon the Prince exercised his ill will by having Lord Randolph and all his family barred from Court.

The term 'garrotters' may mislead. It is the Victorian equiv-alent of 'muggers' and came into use in the mid-nineteenth century as a term for street bandits who robbed their prey by flinging something about the neck and strangling them into submission (or death). In cities where the obviously wealthy lived close to the desperately poor, the practice soon became widespread. A refinement of New York technique involved a dead rat stuffed with lead shot and tied to a length of twine. The operator, a child, would stand at the mouth of some grue-some alley and wait for a likely prospect. The intended victim would see a street child, swinging a revolting homemade toy about its head, and pass on, only to be brought up short when the whirling, weighted rat wrapped firmly about his neck and he was pulled down.

Dublin boasted a unique garrotter known as 'Billy-in-the-Bowl'. Born with seriously crippled legs, Billy made his way about the city seated in a kind of wooden bowl, which he propelled along by thrusting his hands against the pavement. Sometimes he would be seen sprawling out of his bowl, as though it had tipped over and he could not right it. The kindly and unwary would stoop to assist him, only to find themselves fiercely grappled by Billy's arms, made strong by pushing himself about. In a moment they would be robbed of cash or watch or both and Billy would scuttle away aboard his bowl, leaving another victim gasping on the pavement. His nickname passed into Dublin usage as a term for clasping anyone in your arms, hence the lines in the folksong 'The Twang Man's Revenge' – 'He took her down by Sandymount, to watch the waters roll, and he stole the heart of the twang man's mot playing Billy-in-the-Bowl.'

Twenty-Five

The period of Watson's narrative is long before the coming of daily deliveries of bottled milk. In well-served areas (as Burriwell obviously was) there would be two deliveries, in the morning and the early evening, partly because the lack of refrigeration and processing techniques made the keeping of milk difficult. A cart carrying churns of milk would call, and the housewife or a servant would take a jug or a tin milk can to the cart and have it filled with whatever quantity she required.

Twenty-Six

Watson's authenticated records reveal that, in early 1897, Holmes had overtaxed his great strength and was recommended by Watson and by Dr Moore Agar to take a holiday, at the threat of losing his intellectual powers. He travelled to

Cornwall, where he pursued his researches into what he conceived to be the ancient Chaldean roots of the Cornish language, until the matter which Watson chronicled as *The Adventure of the Devil's Foot* occurred.

Since this is a rare occasion when Holmes' client can be definitely identified, it may interest readers to know what became of some of the characters in the story. Holmes himself was, of course, completely uninterested in the later history of his clients, who existed entirely to provide him with intellectual puzzles.

Anna Leonowens returned to Canada, where she died early in the Great War, her funeral being an enormous one. There is an art gallery named after her and she remains a heroine of Canadian feminists. Her book, *The English Governess and the Siamese Court*, was rediscovered in the 1940s, and Margaret Landon's *Anna and the King of Siam* was published. When singing star Gertrude Lawrence saw the film of Landon's book, she wanted to play Anna in a musical version and nagged at Rodgers and Hammerstein to write her one. When they did, it was a huge success on stage and was Lawrence's last part. It became an enormously successful film with Deborah Kerr and Yul Brynner. In 1998 Jodie Foster played Anna in *Anna and the King*, a film which purported to tell the true story and didn't. All the films and Anna's book and Landon's book are banned in modern Thailand (formerly Siam).

King Rama V of Siam, Anna's former pupil Chulalongkorn, reigned until 23rd October 1910, when he died. His death is commemorated annually on that date and he is revered as one of Thailand's most loved and admired monarchs.

None of the points discussed above will prove conclusively whether this narrative is an authentic Watson record or a forgery. I can only argue that the manuscript came to me in the same way as other alleged Watson manuscripts which I have edited. Some of those contain clearer evidence of their authenticity and it seems to me that, if they are authentic, so is the present story. In the end readers must reach their own conclusions.

Barrie Roberts